Lucy Hall Walker Washington

Memory's Casket

Lucy Hall Walker Washington

Memory's Casket

ISBN/EAN: 9783337093013

Printed in Europe, USA, Canada, Australia, Japan

Cover: Foto ©Andreas Hilbeck / pixelio.de

More available books at **www.hansebooks.com**

MEMORY'S CASKET

BY

MRS. LUCY H. WASHINGTON.

———

BUFFALO
CHARLES WELLS MOULTON
1891

WHEN the thoughts, in rhythmic numbers,
  And with rocking cadence flow,
Keeping time to the warm throbbing
  Of Life's pendulum below;
Then the record is a POEM,
  And the oft-recurring rhyme,
Marks its sections, as do figures,
  On the dial-plate of Time.

When the heart breaks forth in rapture,
  Free as flooding light of noon,
And the mind, with jeweled lasso,
  Grasps and holds the glowing tune;
Gives the heart-born captured impulse
  Wings, its mission to prolong,
Bearing love, and cheer, and solace,
  Then the record is a SONG.

When the spirit, earth-environed,
  Seeks the infinite, unknown,
It may catch but dim reflections
  From the glories of God's throne.
Thus the words we blend together,
  From the thoughts that sweetly throng,
Through the soul's creative temple,
  Are but ECHOES OF OUR SONG.

PUBLISHER'S PREFATORY NOTE.

SOME years ago a volume of verse entitled, ECHOES OF SONG, by Mrs. Lucy H. Washington, was issued from the press, and the edition was in a short time exhausted.

In the busy life of the author, as mother, pastor's wife, and one of the foremost of American women in the temperance reform of the last decade, little time has been found for strictly literary work. She has, however, added to her repertory many poems of merit.

At the suggestion of many personal friends this volume has been prepared, embracing selections from ECHOES OF SONG and such other productions of her muse as have found expression in more recent years.

CONTENTS.

POEMS OF PATRIOTISM.

EARLIER POEMS.

POEMS OF MY CHILDREN.

POEMS OF KINDRED.

SUNDAY-SCHOOL SONGS.

POEMS OF TEMPERANCE.

MISCELLANEOUS POEMS.

6 *Contents.*

MEMORY'S CASKET.

I'VE a rare and precious Casket,
  And I only, hold its key;
The bright treasures it encloses,
  Are most sacred now to me;
They are jewels I have gathered,
  All adown the fleeting years;
Some were polished in Life's sunshine,
  Some have sparkled through its tears.

Each was laid away, enfolded
  In sweet lavender of thought;
Each is held within the setting,
  Faithful memory hath wrought;
And the rarest, and the fairest,
  Of this fleeting life of ours,
I have treasured in my Casket,
  With some withered buds and flowers.

Often when I take this Casket,
  And in silence turn the key,
Then a mood, most sweetly solemn,
  Soothingly, comes over me;
As the magic lid is lifted,
  And I view my treasures o'er,
Each one seeming fairer, dearer,
  Than it e'er had been before.

Then the Present seems to vanish,
  And the intervening years
Fade away, as some sweet vision
  Of the LONG AGO appears;

And I clasp hands, true and tender,
  That I ne'er may clasp again,
And the buds burst into blossoms,
  Which so long have withered been.

Then inspiring high Ideal,
  Leads me, in enchanting dream,
Past the rugged living Real,
  Things that are, to things that seem;
Strews the way with rare exotics,
  Builds me castles, grand and fair,—
All suggested by the jewels,
  Treasured with such tender care.

Then I waken to Life's duties,
  Take up all my toil again;
Yet my heart is strengthened, gladdened,
  By the gentle low refrain,
Coming from my magic Casket;
  Song that none but I may hear,
Whispered words of love, and solace,
  Breathèd thoughts of hope and cheer.

O! it is a precious Casket,
  And I only, hold the key,—
No one, while fond mem'ry lingers,
  E'er can take my gems from me;
I alone can know their value,
  With what matchless grace they shine,
I alone behold their beauty,
  Mine they are and only mine.

POEMS OF PATRIOTISM.

BIRTHDAY OF FREEDOM.

USHERED IN BY THE IMMORTAL PROCLAMATION OF OUR MARTYRED PRESIDENT.

HAIL! new birthday of the Nation;
    Of the glorious proclamation;
All our fighting was in vain.
We had learned the lesson slowly,
That we must become more lowly,
    That we must be born again.

Born all free from vile pollution
Of the slave-bound institution,
    Which robs labor of reward.
Evil that hath banished kindness,
Caused secession, madness, blindness,
    Roar of cannon, clash of sword.

All in vain the expiation,
With the fresh blood of the Nation,
    All in vain our strength and might.
We had seen our fate impending,
We were to disruption tending,
    Lest we battle for the right.

.

Since the mighty words were spoken,
" Every bond is hereby broken,
    And our Nation shall be free,"
We, with heart and hand united,
And with faith all newly plighted,
    Have pressed on to victory.

Onward still! ye brave and fearless,
With a cause no longer cheerless;
    Forward march and firmly stand,
In the ranks where noble brothers,
Best beloved of wives and mothers,
    Battle for their native land.

Turn not back, nor yield, nor falter,
If upon thy Country's altar,
    Thou shouldst perish in the strife;
Shrink not, let the Nation's honor—
Freedom, with no stain upon her,
    Be more precious far than life.

Glorious birthday of the Nation!
Faithful, fearless proclamation!
    Weapon forged by powerful hand;
Bravely wielded from this hour,
It shall crush with mighty power,
    Treason throughout all the land.

HOME AGAIN.*

"HOME again!" with thrilling accent,
  Sprang from lips the magic word;
Quickening every pulse and heart throb,
  Where the well-known voice was heard.

Home from war's dark scenes of conflict;
  Home from prison's darker gloom;—
He had thought ere this glad moment,
  To have found a stranger's tomb.

Oh! the torture of those hours,
  Burning hunger, thirst and pain;
Yet he thinks not of their anguish,
  Now that he is *Home* again.

Joyous Frank and gentle Nellie,
  He had greeted just before;
And on either side supported,
  Enters now the open door.

Seeking first, her best beloved,
  Where he finds a glad surprise,
Beaming from each radiant feature,
  Glancing from those up-turned eyes.

---

*Suggested by the beautiful picture, "Home Again," painted by
TREVOR McCLURG, Esq., of Pittsburgh, Penn.

Him, the idol of the maiden;
  Dearest treasure of the wife;
She with loyal heart had yielded,
  For the Nation's trembling life.

What glad tumult fills her bosom!
  Recompense for waiting pain,
For the land she loves is rescued,
  Whom she gave is *Home* again.

Mother, name scarce less endearing,
  Manifests maternal joy,
As she stands in mute thanksgiving,
  That God hath restored her boy.

Others called him Captain, Colonel,
  Even General though he be,
She but sees her noble Edward,
  Merry boy of yesterday.

Father gravely waits a greeting;
  Age hath silvered o'er his hair,
Else he too had joined the conflict;
  For his heart had followed there.

All are joyous at his coming,
  'Tis a cheerful happy sight;
Even Carlo bounding forward
  Plainly shows a dog's delight.

Only one is shy and doubting,
  Little prattling Baby May;
She has learned to lisp of Papa,
  Yet she knows him not to-day.

Yes, it is a gladsome picture,
  Yet with joy it giveth pain,
When we think of precious thousands,
  Never to come *Home* again.

*   *   *   *   *   *   *   *   *

God protect our rescued Country,
  From her foes, where'er they stand,
Whether in her halls of council,
  Or with wielded sword in hand.

Let the blood of perished heroes
  Wash away each darkling stain,
And the glorious light of Freedom,
  Never be obscured again.

THE SOLDIER'S ORPHAN.

"HAVE you any money mother?"
    Whispered dying Frankie Bly;
"Who'll take care of baby brother
    And of you; but Fred and I?

"Now I'm sick, and cannot carry
    Daily papers any more,
Mother, you must need more money,
    Surely than you did before.

"Who'll get Eddie a warm tippet,
    Who'll get Nellie her new shoes,
Since I'm sick, and cannot carry
    Any more the 'Daily News'?

"Father made us such nice presents,
    'Old Chris' sent them all, he said,
But you know he never sends them,
    Since dear Father has been dead.

"You remember when he 'listed,
    Father said, if he should die,
We must care for you and baby,
    Be brave boys, and never cry.

" When he talked, as he was dying,
  And they couldn't understand,
Don't you think he said that ' Frankie
  Will be mother's little man ? '

" Don't cry mother; when I'm better,
  I will help you all the more,
And we'll have a Merry Christmas,
  Just as we have had before."

But the little Hero brother,
  In an hour had passed away;
Heaven help the stricken Mother,
  And the rest, on Christmas day.

" *VICTORY.*"

ALAS! alas! for our bleeding land;
  There is sorrow and mourning on every hand;
For all our grand triumphs, so valiant to gain,
Sad tears of bereavement are falling like rain:
O, remember each fallen, each patriot son,
When ye shout with glad voices, " The victory won."

OUR MARTYRED PRESIDENT.*

MOURN for the Chief of the Nation, who
perished
  By the assassin's demoniac hand;
One whom we had chosen, and honored and cher-
    ished,
  Whose blood sealed the clasp o'er Columbia's
    land.

PRAISE—for oppression is banished forever,
  Her dark reign is over from river to sea;
In truth and in spirit, as now, sang we never,
  "Of the land of the brave, and the home of the
    free."

Our God, who in wisdom the dark strife permitted,—
  Though the bow was obscured in the midst of
    the storm;
Now war clouds are broken, and vengeance requited,
  Shows the wonders, He worketh, His will to
    perform.

Then boast not of conquest, or wisdom; but chided,
  In contrite submission and penitence bowed,

---

*Suggested by the Dedication of the NATIONAL LINCOLN MONUMENT,
at Springfield, Ill., October 15, 1874.

Give thanks to the Lord, who our armies hath
    guided,
  For '' Why should the spirit of mortal be proud ? ''

Yet long as our banner shall wave in her beauty;—
  As long as we sing of the red, white and blue;
Columbia will honor in pleasure and duty,
  The memory of LINCOLN, brave, honest and true.

Assembled to-day are the pride of the Nation,
  Surrounding the spot where his hallowed dust lies;
Reviewing his service in grandest oration,
  Recording his virtues in loftiest praise.

Though granite and bronze tower high where he
    sleepeth,
  A nation's bereavement and grief, to proclaim;
More lasting and precious the love-light that keepeth,
  Enshrined in the hearts of the people, his name.

OUR COUNTRY.

*READ BEFORE THE LITERARY SOCIETIES OF CEN-
TRAL UNIVERSITY, PELLA, IOWA, JUNE, 1876.*

OF the History of Nations,
   Which upon Time's page appears,
There is one whose life is numbered,
   Only by a hundred years.
This we claim as mother country,
   And she challenges to-day,
All the world to view the wonders,
   Of our land of Liberty.

It becomes us who are living,
   In this educating age,
To trace carefully the verdict,
   On this written, changeless page;
Striving to work out the problem,
   How, 'midst earthly care and strife,
We may serve the noblest purpose,
   Of a brief allotted life.

We are called a working people;
   There is honor in the name;
We could ask for nothing better,
   In the calendar of Fame.
"Work for Right," upon our banners,
   O'er the land should be unfurled,

And our works should represent us,
  Men and women, to the world.

Shall we tarry for a moment,
  Very briefly to relate,
How prosperity hath crowned us,
  In each blood-bought, star-bound state?
How our favored land has blossomed,
  And her rich prolific soil,
Hath abundant harvest yielded,
  To repay the tillers' toil?

Her broad lakes and winding rivers,
  On their sun-kissed tide have borne
Freight, which brings into her coffers,
  Wealth abundant, in return.
Her grand hills are stored with treasure,
  And her caverns, deep and low,
Have burst forth with oil of gladness,
  Light and comfort to bestow.

In this great and growing nation,
  Very justly we take pride;
And rejoice in the progression
  Manifest on every side.
Towering churches, spacious mansions,
  Meet the eye on either hand,
While her stately HALLS OF LEARNING,
  Rise in grandeur o'er the land.

Monuments of spotless marble,
　　Towering heavenward, proclaim
Where our honored dead are lying,
　　Who have won undying fame.
Some have fought our battles for us,
　　And have perished in the strife,
Thus bequeathing to the nation
　　Sacred trust, with precious life.

As we meet to scatter blossoms
　　Where our fallen soldiers lie,
May we prize the gift of Freedom,
　　Boon for which they dared to die.
And from Lincoln's tomb of grandeur,
　　To the humblest unknown grave,
May we honor all the fallen,
　　Who have died their land to save.

Countless multitudes are thronging
　　To our land, from o'er the sea;
Beckoned by the glowing pictures
　　Of our "Home of Liberty."
Many who are slaves of passion,
　　In dark bondage unto sin,
Bringing all their fetters with them—
　　Still, they freely enter in.

Some have brought their king, Gambrinus,
　　And are planting on our sod,
Training schools which now are leading
　　Anywhere but unto God.

While the blighting shadows deepen
  Over Utah's distant plain,—
Ignorance and superstition
  Gathered from across the main.

Do we glory in our triumphs?
  Let it be with modest grace,
Not forgetting the dark shadows
  Which remain yet to efface,
Ere our land among the nations
  Stands as honest, brave and true,
With a band of fearless rulers
  And no liquor revenue.

Not alone into the hovel,
  Stalks the demon of the night;
It is found within the mansion,
  With its dark and withering blight.
Here, one reared in degradation
  Is borne on the seething tide,—
There, a fainting, struggling victim,
  From the ranks of wealth and pride.

Is a tower less a prison,
  For its gilded burnished dome?
Is the palace barricaded
  Where this evil may not come?
While the lowest of the lowest,
  Sink into the drunkard's grave,
It has also claimed the noble,
  And the bravest of the brave.

Shall we boast our Schools of Science,
    Blended with ennobling art?
Shall we boast our land of Freedom,
    Dear to every patriot heart,
While we harbor in our borders,
    Schools which train our youth in vice,—
Schools protected by the people,
    Chartered, licensed, for a price?

Shall we say to liquor dealers,
    As all license truly saith:
"Share with us your purchase money,
    And deal out the dole of death?"
Shall we hold the reeling victim,
    Till he stands upon his feet,
To be lured into the dram shop,
    And make ruin more complete?

Many brave and fearless heroes,
    Gave their lives our land to save;
We have passed Charybdis' vortex,
    Must we sink 'neath Scylla's wave?
Let us rally to the rescue,
    Meet this tyrant of the bowl,
Who is holding slaves by thousands,
    Fettered heart and hand and soul!

Freedom's grandest gift, the franchise,
    Tarnish not by spot or stain,
Sell it not for price or party,
    Give it not for greed or gain.

When each voter, in the ballot
  Seeks the people's greatest good,
Then the mighty voice of franchise,
  Shall proclaim true brotherhood.

Aid no wrong, for price or party,
  Is a law of life and love;
Have no fellowship with evil,
  Said our Savior, but reprove.
All the tide that leads to ruin,
  Though we may not, cannot stay,
Shall our "bonds approved," and "licensed,"
  Speed the deluge on its way?

Ladies hold your power not lightly,
  Spurn the patron of the bowl;
Shun the wine, and the wine-bibber,
  As you value life and soul.
If you cannot hold a lover
  To a sober upright life,
Do not trust your power to rescue,
  In the higher sphere of wife.

What will maiden charms avail you,
  To make beautiful the home,
Where the senseless, maddened drunkard,
  To its sacred shrines must come?
He may furnish you a palace,
  Decked by aid of every art,
But he never can afford you,
  A true temple for the heart.

By the homes we so much cherish,
   For our daughters, fair and true,
And our sons so brave and noble,
   May we all this pledge renew..
That we will go bravely forward
   In each heaven-appointed way,
With voice of love, and power of ballot,
   This dark pestilence to stay.

With the grandly closing cycle
   Of the waning century,
Rounded now since our forefathers
   Raised the flag of Liberty;—
May we sign a declaration,
   Independent of the power,
That is holding this great nation
   In such bondage at this hour.

Then, the 'victims of base passion,
   May rejoice as they go free;
And the song shall be repeated,
   From the rivers to the sea;
And from mountain-top to mountain,
   · There shall swell an anthem high,—
Anthem that shall be re-echoed
   From the ramparts of the sky;
When our nation works to further
   Heaven's great redemptive plan,
Proving that her grand incentive,
   Is man's love for fellow man.

BURIAL OF PRESIDENT GARFIELD.

TOLL! solemn bells; toll! toll!
   Proclaim the nation's dole,
Let sorrow's anthem roll,
   Deep-toned and grand.
Beat! muffled drums; O beat!
While slow responsive feet,
A funeral train complete
   Throughout our land.

Trail, trail your banners low,
That all the world may know,
A nation's grief and woe,
   On this sad day.
The hero of our trust,
A noble man, and just,
Is borne to kindred dust,
   In mortal clay.

Closed every business mart;
The nation's throbbing heart,
This day may have no part
   In strife for gain.
The rain of falling tears,
Proclaim how love endears,
Through changing hopes and fears,
   Our noble slain.

The honored, weary form,
That bravely faced each storm,
With heart true, loving, warm,
   Lay gently down;
Called from our nation's mast,
Life's conflicts all are passed,
Our chief hath won at last
   A fadeless crown.

Bow low, in humble prayer,
And ask the loving care,
Of Him who did not spare
   His only son;
O God of nations! lead,
In this our hour of need;
In His loved name we plead
   "Thy will be done."

EARLIER POEMS.

CHRIST UPON THE WATERS.

THICK and fast the rain is falling
   Over Palestine at night;
And the darkness is illumined
   By the lightning's lurid light;
And the silent hour is broken
   By the distant thunder's roar,—
Watch-word of the mighty storm-king,
   Which resounds from shore to shore.

Ere the winds had roused the billows,
   Ere the shadows gathered dark,
Saw ye far upon the waters,
   Gently float a fragile bark?
Now, alas! 'tis wildly driven
   Onward, by the hurrying blast,
Now its sails are rent asunder,
   Now the trusty anchor cast.

Yet those hardy seamen tremble,
   At the thunder's crashing roar,
For their boat is tossing wildly,
   Still more wildly than before;

Aye! their hearts are chilled with terror,
   Where is now the power to save,
For the sea is lashed to fury,
   Must they sink beneath the wave?

While the billows rage around them,
   And the clouds burst overhead,
The disciples are reminded
   Of the Master, in their dread,
And they hasten to awake Him:
   " Rouse Thee Master! or we die—
Car'st Thou not that we should perish,
   For the tempest rageth high."

He arises, stands beside them,
   Gently bids them " Fear no more;"
Still the lightnings flash around them,
   Still the sullen thunders roar.
List! unto the raging billows
   Jesus speaketh, " Peace be still,"
And the storm is hushed to silence,
   For the winds obey His will.

Thus may we, when earthly billows
   Surge around the frightened soul,
Baffling all the sails of purpose,
   Rending anchors of control;
Go and call upon the Master,
   He will hear an earnest cry,
And will rescue those who trust Him,
   When life's tempest rageth high.

LIGHT AND LOVE.

IT was sunset hour,
  And the magic power
Of the golden skies serene,
  Fell on all around,
  As in thought, spell-bound,
I gazed upon the scene.

  I beheld a cloud,
  And its mien was proud
As it towered o'er earth so high;
  For its form was light,
  And its face was bright,
And it hung in the clear blue sky.

  As I gazed with joy
  On Heaven's fair toy,
I beheld a gradual change;
  The cloud still there,
  Yet no longer fair,
And I thought, 'tis passing strange;

  Till I glanced again
  On Heaven's blue plain,
And saw that its tint grew deep;
  For the orb of day,
  With his brilliant ray,
Had sunk in the west to sleep.

And then I knew
'Twas that he withdrew,
That my cloud was no longer bright;
For its brilliant shade
Had been portrayed,
By his all-reflecting light.

There is a light
Which is still more bright,
'Twill the fairest hues impart;
It comes from above,
'Tis the light of love,`
And it beautifies the heart.

It strews the path
Of the child of Earth,
With fair unfading flowers;
And with pencil bright,
In their rapid flight,
It gilds the passing hours.

Yet unlike the sun
When his course is run,
Who is followed by darksome night;
For the fount of love,
Is in Heaven above,
Where it shineth ever bright.

A SONG OF CHANGE,

OR, AN OLD MAN'S SOLILOQUY.

THERE'S a cot that I loved in my childhood,
    And 'tis cherished by memory still,
Nestled down by a deep-shady wildwood,
    At the foot of a far sloping hill;
Roses sweet grew beside the low window,
    And a woodbine twined over the door,
Flowers, fresher, or fairer, or dearer,
    Shall blossom for me nevermore.

There's a brook that I loved in my childhood,
    And it ripples in memory still,
Hiding oft in the midst of the wildwood,
    As it winds round the foot of the hill.
Graceful willows droop lovingly o'er it,
    And its waters are crystal and clear,
And the pebbles that sparkle beneath them—
    Bright rubies were never so dear.

There's a form that I loved in my childhood,
    And most sacred to memory still;
My dear mate as I roamed through the wildwood,
    Near the cot at the foot of the hill.
O! her eye was as blue and as gentle
    As the sky, which smiled over us then,
And a voice so enchanting and bird-like,
    I shall listen to—never again.

There's a hope that I cherished in childhood,
  In my dreams it revisits me still,
As I wander again in the wildwood,
  As I dwell in the cot by the hill.
This sweet hope, how it gladdens the future,
  Where the path of my life is all bright,
For a gentle one lingers beside me,
  Even down to its shadowy night.

But alas for my dreary awakings!
  Into darkness, not dawning they seem;
Oh, would that my dreamings were real,
  And my life's cheerless journey a dream.
But time has brought many sad changes,
  With burdens of labor and care,
While years in their ceaseless returnings,
  Have whitened to silver, my hair.

The cot that I loved in my childhood
  Has fallen from final decay;
Vanished the dear shady wildwood,
  The woodman has cut it away.
The brook, by whose banks I have sported,
  Is mournfully murmuring still;
The form, and the hope, that I cherished,
  Are asleep on the side of the hill.

ANGEL LISTENERS.

WHEN the Night her plumes are spreading,
   Slowly o'er her sable nest,
And the weary, and the careworn,
   Sink in quietude to rest;
'Tis delightful then to fancy,
   When the evening prayer is said,
That the angels gladly listen,
   Hovering near us, overhead.

Every feeble, faint petition,
   Finds a welcome mid the throng;
And they bear it gently upward,
   Praising as they float along,
That the power to them is given,
   Thus to minister to man,
Sweetly singing richest praises
   For the world's redeeming plan.

Though the shadows round us gather,
   Still the angels bask in light;
Aye! we hear them chant of Heaven.
   Where is neither shade, nor night.
If the heart be faint and weary,
   Angel voices murmur low,
Of a land, all free from sorrow—
   Of a rest we soon shall know.

List! they whisper words of promise,
  As they linger near at even,
Waiting to be joyous bearers,
  Of repentant thoughts to Heaven.
And it soothes the heart to fancy
  That mid shades of life's dark night,
They will bear the spirit heavenward,
  To the realms of endless light.

JUDSON'S GRAVE.
1851.

HE had borne the rod,
  He had taught of God,
Through him was a nation bless'd;
  Though the ocean now,
  Rolls o'er his brow,
Yet sweet is his tranquil rest.

  'Neath the drifting wave,
  Is the " Teacher's " grave,
Where none may e'er repair,
  With a loving heart,
  To bestow in part,
Affection's offerings there.

  Yet with all that sleep,
  In the mighty deep,
At the great Archangel's tread,
  He will early rise,
  To the joyous skies,
When the sea gives up its dead.

TO A BROWN THRUSH.

BEAUTIFUL, beautiful, forest bird,
 Dost thou tarry to sing unto me?
Gladly thy clear woodland voice is heard,
 Trilling so wild and free.

Hast thou paused in thy flight, on this oaken tree,
 Ere far o'er the fields thou shalt roam,
To carol a welcoming song for me,
 To make brighter my western home?

Dost thou come, sweet bird, with thy cheering song,
 From some feathered throng on high?
Dost thou gather the hues of thy graceful form,
 From the light of a western sky?

O linger, dear bird, 'neath my window awhile,
 There is power in thy mellow tone
To banish the tear, which, displaced by a smile,
 Will return, if thou leav'st me alone.

Alas! thou hast flown, far away, far away;
 Still my heart will remember thee long;
Remember, at parting, thou seem'dst to say,
 'Gather fragments of sunshine and song.''

TWILIGHT.

E ARTH is beautiful, 'tis eventide;
     My heart is filled with naught beside
     The loveliness of eve.
Adieu, yon pale retreating light,
Being less welcome far than night,
     Well takest thou thy leave.

And thou, great glorious orb of day,
Through Heaven's arch hast sped thy way,
     Sole parentage of light.
Thy couch with crimson thou hast dressed,
And seemingly hath sunk to rest,—
     Thou too, dost welcome night.

Yon star that loves not brilliant day,
Comes forth to shed its tiny ray,
     As if with thought impressed.
It twinkles o'er those towering trees,
Whose foliage whispers to the breeze,—
     Hush, 'tis the hour of rest.

I list, and hear the gushing rills;
The cattle on the sloping hills
     Are silent in repose.

With joy they hailed the opening day,
Which quietly they've grazed away,—
    With gratitude, its close.

Light fleecy clouds of mellow hue,
Sink nearer earth, and gentle dew,
    As grateful off'ring bring.
Each bird is hushed in tree and bower,
To enjoy the shadowy twilight hour,
    With head beneath its wing.

How sweetly died its evening song,
Which echo, anxious to prolong,
    Endeavored to repeat.
'Twere vain, she could not sing so well,
And yet there was a magic spell
    About her music, sweet.

A spell that wraps my soul in love,
That raised my thoughts, my heart above,
    In gratitude and prayer.
If such fair scenes to us are given,
Such music lent to earth from Heaven,
    What are the glories there?

My heart beats not in tumult wild,
With impulse caused by Nature's smile,
    There's sadness on her brow.
And yet that sadness is so sweet,
I, glad in mine own spirit, greet
    Her gentle teachings now.

Methinks there is an unseen power,
Hovering o'er earth at twilight hour
    That lulls the mind to rest.
So when the night of life draws near,
Kind spirit, quell each doubt and fear
    That lingers in the breast.

POEMS OF MY CHILDREN.

THE FIRST BORN.

IRVING.

IS this *my* little baby boy,
　　That nestles by my side,
That fills my heart with gladsome joy?
　　Nay, do not call it pride—
With joy, I ne'er before have known,
　　That unto me is given,
A little treasure all my own,
　　Just from the courts of Heaven.

A few brief days upon time's tide
　　My little one has known,
His fragile barque he could not guide,
　　Upon its waves alone.
And so secured beside mine own,
　　He floats without a fear,
And who shall say he does not know,
　　Some guiding hand is near?

Yet thus it may not ever be,
　　For when long years have passed,

And I, with failing strength, shall near
 The distant shore at last—
When firm at helm, with manhood's power,
 My child shall stem the tide,
Perhaps his mother's barque will float,
 Securely by his side.

He's sleeping now, yet mark his face,
 And see those dimples play;
What sees my little darling one?
 What do the angels say?
'Tis said when sleeping infants smile,
 That unto them 'tis given,
To see the smiling angel bands,
 Who tune their harps in Heaven.

Delightful thought, and why not true?
 Did not the Savior say,
" Of such as these my kingdom is,
 Then turn them not away? "
O Father, grant this gift of thine,
 Kept free from every stain,
May, by a pure and spotless life,
 Return Heaven's smiles again.

LOANED.

EDWARD.

ONLY a cherub loaned,
  Love to enfold;
Only a little stay,
  Earth to behold.

Plumed for the " Happy Land,"
  Radiant and bright,
Our darling so precious
  Has taken his flight.

Why should'st thou linger,
  On life's troubled sea,
When the angels, dear Eddie,
  Were waiting for thee?

CHILDREN'S PHILOSOPHY.

IT was night, and the rain fell in torrents,
   Sharp lightnings flashed down from on high;
Then deep thunders rolled in the darkness,
   When Mattie peered up toward the sky,

And there, saw a scene of such grandeur,
   Of lightning and darkness in strife,
As she had not seen to remember,
   In all the four years of her life.

Her lips were half-parted in wonder,
   Her eyes opened wide with surprise,
As she listened to rain and to thunder,
   And gazed out with awe to the skies.

Then quickly she turned to us, smiling;
   In thought, a solution had come:
"Oh listen! dear Mamma, in heaven,
   The Lord is just beating his drum."

"No, daughter," the mother made answer,
   "The Lord has no drum in the skies."
Then the mouth opened wider with wonder,
   The eye showed still greater surprise.

She pondered in doubt but a moment,
   A reason occurred to her soon,

And she said, "Then I spect up in heaven
The Lord must be striking the moon."

Then Irving, of eight, spoke up boldly,
With wisdom, concerning the weather;
"Why! Mattie! I thought you knew better!
The *clouds are just bumping together.*"

WHERE IS HEAVEN?

"MAMMA," said a little prattler,
   "Where is Heaven?" "Far away,"
Dreamily the mother answered,
   Wondering what she *ought* to say;
When the little infant skeptic
   Who believed, where he could see,
Said, "Is it beyond the hilltop—
   And the clouds above the tree?"
"Yes," the mother faintly answered.
   "And beyond the moon, so high?"
"Yes." "And, Mamma, will you surely
   Go to Heaven when you die?"
"Mamma hopes to," said she meekly;
   Then the darling ran away.
And the mother pondered over
   Questions he had asked that day.
But, the question was not settled,
   For her boy returning soon
Said, "Why Mamma! such big lady
   Could *not* get *behind the moon!*"

LUCY MAY.

H AVE you seen our Lucy May?
    Have you seen the darling, say?
O! but she is wondrous fair,
With the silken chestnut hair,
Curling round her cherub head,
While her dainty lips so red,
Ever seem to ask a kiss,
And our hearts are filled with bliss,
Since she cheers us every day,
Precious baby, Lucy May.

She has such a cunning nose,
And her cheeks are like the rose,
While her brow is lily fair,
'Neath the curling chestnut hair.
Stars within the folds of night,
Never shone with purer light,
Than her little love-lit eyes,
Speaking, giving sweet replies,
And bright smiles, like sunbeams play,
On the face of Lucy May.

Ne'er was princess' jeweled wand,
Charming as her dimpled hand.
How we cheered with rapturous joy,
Her first grasp of tiny toy;—

Now she hides her eyes from view,
Glances out, for "Peek-a-boo."
She can make a "patty cake,"
"Pick it, toss it up to bake,"
And more wondrous still than this,
She can throw a honey-kiss.
Winsome baby, Lucy May,
Mother's wonder all the day.

Yet, oh why those dewy tears,
As I glance adown the years,
On the battle-field of life?
Baby May must join the strife,
Bravely may she share its toil.
She may meet its wild turmoil,—
Darling cannot always rest
On a loving mother's breast.
Heavenly Father, grant this prayer,
May she have Thy tender care;
Safely o'er life's changing way,
Guard, and guide, our Lucy May.

JOY AND SORROW.

EMMA.

APRIL 10, 1870.

PASS'D were the shadows of the night,
    The bird-hailed morn had come;
Life's angel tarried in his flight,
    To leave within our home
A little cherub, whose dear life
    Should ever more entwine,
In scenes of joy, or sorrow's strife,
    So tenderly with mine.

Blossoms are springing to the light,
    Buds bursting on the tree,
All nature singing with delight,
    As this life comes to me.
May not our precious little bud,
    By her sweet presence, bring
Love's warmth, and sunshine, to abide,
    Like a perpetual spring?

I clasp a clinging rose-tint hand,
    And on her lips and brow,
Press pledges of the mother love,
    Which gushes freshly now.
And then in musing, dreamy mood,
    Through mists of tender tears,

I try to picture out her life,
In all those coming years.

But thus it wisely may not be;
He who my darling gave,
Alone can trace her pathway, from
The cradle to the grave.
To Him who doeth all things well,
I breathe a mother's prayer,
· And trust the dear one by my side,
To His protecting care.

JULY 10, 1871.

Well might I not discern the way!
A few brief months had sped,
When our wee star that dawned with day,
With evening shadows fled;
And we are left in sorrow's night,
Whose density is riven,
By that firm faith, eluding sight,
Which opes the gates of Heaven.

The Shepherd saw our precious lamb,
That she was chilled with cold;
He clasped her little waxen hand,
And bore her to His fold,
Where turbid flood, and raging storm,
Can never, never come,
To fright our darling, or to cast
A shadow o'er her home.

BABY'S EYES.

NELLY.

D EAR little eyes, beautiful eyes,
  Winking and blinking, with queer surprise,
Now peeping at you, now peering at me;
What do you think, can the little one see,   •
  With the wee starry eyes,
   Which like windows are given,
   To look through on earth,
   From the borders of heaven?

Little bright eyes, light giving eyes!
How bless'd are the beings on whom they arise!
'Tis cheerless without, frost-bound and so drear,
What matter? within is all sparkling with cheer.
   And all from the light
   Of the sweet baby's eyes.
   Alas! for the homes
   Where such lights never rise.

Little brown eyes, wonderful eyes!
What do we see in the marvelous eyes?
Treasure more precious than silver or gold,—
Fathoms of love, that can never be told,—
   Adding beauty to earth,
   Leading up to the skies;
   That's what we see
   In the dear baby's eyes.

MY SLEEPING BABES.

I HAVE come once more in sadness,
    To weep o'er precious dust;
I have come once more with gladness,
    And a firm, abiding trust;
For I know my babes, though sleeping,
    'Neath the sunlit stars, or rain,
Are safe in my Savior's keeping,
    He will give them back again.

Oh! how keen the bitter anguish,
    When my lovely infant boy,
In my clinging arms must languish,
    While I tried so to employ,
Aid of every known appliance,
    His most precious life to save,—
When had failed all skill, and science,
    I must yield him to the grave.

With what eagerness I pleaded
    For the life of my dear son,
Adding, in the faintest whisper,
    "Not my will, but Thine be done."
And when life's last ray had flickered,
    It seemed almost hard to say,
"Blessed be the Hand that gave him
    And—hath taken now away."

As I robed my mute, cold darling,
    For his long earth-cradled rest,
Placed the buds within the waxen,
    Dimpled hands, upon his breast;
Bathed the face, in death so lovely,
    With a mother's tenderest tears;
Then, I thought to keep my sorrow,
    Fresh through all the coming years.

Years have passed since last I clasped him
    To my aching, throbbing breast;
Longing to embalm the casket,
    In love's clinging, fond caress;
And as I am strewing blossoms
    O'er his restful grave to-day,
I can add with firmer accent,
    "And hath taken him away."

*   *   *   *   *   *

Once again the shadow rested
    On our home, so bless'd with light.
Once again we were enveloped
    In the gloom of sorrow's night.
But we turned us from the casket,
    Lovely form, and snowy shroud,
To the promise of the Father,
    "There is light beyond the cloud."

Thorns we've found along life's pathway,
    Ne'er can pierce their tender feet,
While our rest has oft been broken,
    Theirs has tranquil been, and sweet.

Should the darkest earth-storms gather,
    They are safe from all alarms,
And I bless the gentle Savior
    Who has borne them in His arms.

As I read upon the marble,
    Names we called our darlings by;
As I whisper, "Eddie," "Emma,"
    Listening vainly for reply,
I look up, and sweetly fancy,
    That they heed the voice of love,
Though my babes may only answer,
    To the angel roll above.

OAK RIDGE CEMETERY, SPRINGFIELD, ILL., April, 1872.

A LOCK OF SILVER HAIR.

1859.

I HAVE shorn away from my Mother's brow,
  A lock of silver hair, '
And I think, as I gaze on the token now,
  When that brow was young and fair.

This lock was then of a chestnut hue,
  And her hopes of life were bright.
I ask my heart, are they faded too,
  As the tress has grown so white?

Some years ago, a tender form
  She clasped to her loving breast,
And she longed to shield from every storm,
  The child to her bosom pressed.

She pictured a life all bright and fair,
  As she toyed with the hand that now
Hath shorn this shining tress of hair,
  From her pale and care-worn brow.

She says that the days have fleetly passed,
  And that in review, they seem

Like a changing scene, that could not last,
Like a varied transient dream.

" And thus," she says, "it will be with you,
For ere you are aware,
The locks that are now of chestnut hue,
Will change to silver hair.

" Life's mingled scenes, in their rapid flight,
Will wear a somber hue,
While the densely dark, or the gaily bright,
That greet thee, will be but few.

" Then, remember dear, when the night is dark,
Or when morn is exceeding fair,—
' Tis a changing sea, with an earthly barque,—
Remember the silver hair."

*   *   *   *   *   *

That shining tress, so dear to me,
Twined with my own to-night
But verifies her prophecy,
For both are silver white.

MY MOTHER'S LAST BLESSING.

1863.

THE sands of life, my children,
  Are slowly ebbing now;
And while death's chilling dampness
  Is stealing o'er my brow,
While this fond heart is beating,
  Ere the tender chord be riven,
That binds me to this earthly sphere,
  And keeps me back from heaven—
A mother's parting blessing,
  I hasten to bestow,
On those so fondly cherished,
  Who must tarry here below.

Take up cheerfully life's burdens,
  With a firm, courageous heart,
And in all Time's changing drama
  Act an earnest, faithful part.
Strive to serve the lowly Master;
  Let thy watchword ever be—
I will labor for the Savior,
  Who hath lived and died for me.
Oh! 'tis sweet to know the Shepherd
  Ever hath a tender care,
For all those who love, and trust Him,
  And their paths He will prepare.

Follow wheresoe'er He leadeth,
　Whether on the mountain high,
Or, perchance, low in the valley,
　Where the shadows thickly lie.
Ever joyful in life's sunshine,
　And when her dark sorrows come,
Let them prove a sweet reminder
　Of that brighter, better home,
Where no sorrow e'er can enter,
　Where is neither shade, nor night,
Where bless'd spirits dwell forever,
　In the realms of endless light.

Oh! my heart is thrilled with pleasure,
　Though its pulses feebly beat,
When I think of the departed,
　Whom, with joy, I soon shall greet.
From the brink of Death's dark river,
　I discern the "Shining shore,"
I am waiting now, and watching,
　Till the angels bear me o'er.
List! I hear the voices calling,
　And must hasten to bestow
A last blessing on the loved ones,
　Who must linger here below.

NEARING THE RIVER.*

"I will fear no evil, for Thou art with me."

FEAR not! for lo, I am with thee,
    On the brink of Death's dark flood,
To prepare the way before thee,
    And thy passport is My blood.
All the darkness is but shadow,
    Hiding Canaan's shore from view;
I have crossed the surging billow,
    And will bear thee safely through.

Unseen beauties, untold raptures,
    Wait thee on the other side;
Thou shalt look with glad thanksgiving,
    On the dim receding tide,
Which has borne thee from all sorrow,
    From a world of pain, and care,
To the realms of bliss eternal,
    For there is no sorrow there.

Dearest sister, may we ever
    To the great Redeemer live,
Whether with fresh-throbbing pulses,
    Which new life and vigor give;
Or, with weary, fainting spirit,
    We await the Master's will,—
They that labor for Him, serve Him,
    Those who suffer, serve Him still.

* To my sister Myra, shortly before her death, March 14, 1865.

FOUR SCORE.

*TO MY FATHER ON HIS EIGHTIETH BIRTHDAY, CEL-
EBRATED AT DARTFORD, WIS., JULY 15, 1879.*

OLD Time has numbered years four score
　　Since launched upon life's tide,
There was an infant　ark which bore
　　The hero by my side.

In far away New England home,
　　Fond parents found the—"Moses,"
Not left to toss and die unknown,
　　But anchored 'mid life's roses.

Glad children gathered round to see,
　　The wondrous new-found treasure,
And clapped their hands in merry glee,
　　Expressive of their pleasure.

The neighboring wives soon "happened round,"
　　And were surprised—it may be,
To find within their thriving town
　　So wonderful a baby.

For, while each child had seemed complete,
　　The last was the completest;
While each one in its way was sweet,
　　The youngest was the sweetest.

No palace walls this baby knew,
　Beheld no regal splendor;
But in the cottage where he grew,
　Was true love, warm and tender.

Piano there you could not find,
　But birds gave sweetest singing;
While woodmen in the chorus joined,
　With trusty axes ringing.

'Twas thus, four score of years ago,
　New England homes were "cleared;"
When stately forests were laid low,
　And sons and daughters "reared."

Simple supply, met simple need,
　And by the hearthstone altar,
They worshipped God—held simple creed,
　And faith that did not falter.

To manhood, soon, my hero grew,
　But I must hasten over
The years that all so swiftly flew,
　Past schoolboy, youth and lover.

'Twas by a fireside of his own
　That I first chanced to meet him,—
Came from the wonderland alone,
　One early morn to greet him.

The winds were blowing cold and bleak,
　The wintry snow was falling

That morn, when I with tiny feet,
So early came a calling.

They gave the little stranger room,
Proclaimed there was another
To share the tender care of home,
The love of father—mother.
* * * * * *
And I, that child of years ago,—
(At home, a child again,)
Take up the lyre I sometimes use
To join in the refrain,

Which memory of the bygone years,
This day is freshly bringing,—
Ah! there are strains for joy and tears
In life songs we are singing.

Belovèd ones are not all here,
Yet as we praise The Giver,
We almost catch the echoed cheer,
Of those beyond the river.

Some that remain, upon this day,
With grateful gladness gather,
This tribute of respect to pay
To our devoted father.

Long years of life lie in the rear,
And in the days before him,
May Faith, and Love, and Hope and Cheer
Bear all their banners o'er him.

And may we all, when life is past,
   Be gathered at the river,
Launched for the " Summer Land " at last,
   There to abide forever.

*   *   *   *   *   *

SEPTEMBER, 1879.

AT REST.

At rest! our dear Father;
Heaven's angels of slumber,
Have tenderly called thee to peaceful repose.
The record is ended,
Four score is the number
To mark thy long life, at its evening close.

WORK TO DO FOR JESUS.

MUSIC BY REV. ROBERT LOWRY.

"The harvest truly is plenteous, but the laborers are few."

THERE is work to do for Jesus,
   Yes, a glorious work to do,
For a harvest fully ripened,
   Rich and golden, lies in view.
With a prayer to God, our Father,
   Let us all the work pursue,
For our risen Lord is calling,
   And the harvesters are few.

CHORUS.

Yes, there's work to do for Jesus,
   And the harvest is in view,
There's a great work everywhere to do;
There is work to do for Jesus,
   And the harvesters are few,
There's enough work for all to do.

There is work to do for Jesus,
   And we hear the Savior say,
"Why art standing here so idle,
   At the noontide, on the way?

Even now I will accept thee;
　With the rest, thy wages pay;
Go and labor in My vineyard,
　Till the closing of the day.''

CHORUS—

Yes, there's work to do for Jesus,
　Who will answer to the call?
See! the vintage is abundant,
　There is work to do for all.
God commands that we should labor,
　Though the task our hearts appall,
For He claimeth our life-service,
　Till the shades of death shall fall.

CHORUS.

Yes, there's work to do for Jesus,
　And the harvest is in view,
There's a great work everywhere to do.
There is work to do for Jesus,
　And the harvesters are few,
There's enough work for all to do.

NEVER FORGET.

MUSIC BY PROF. J. W. BISCHOFF.

"Behold, I stand at the door, and knock."

NEVER forget that the SAVIOR is near,
    Asking if thou wilt receive Him;
He will protect, from all danger and fear,
    Those who love, trust and believe Him.

CHORUS.

Never forget, never forget
Jesus is near, oh! receive Him.
He will come in, banish all sin,
Cheerfully trust, and believe Him.

Never forget that the MASTER is near,
    All of thy life He is viewing,
How shall the record before Him appear,
    Art thou His precepts pursuing?

CHORUS—

Never forget the GOOD SHEPHERD is near,
    Patiently leading, and guiding;
Turn not away, lest His voice thou shalt hear,
    Tenderly pleading, and chiding.

CHORUS—

Never forget the REDEEMER is near,
Nor the dear ransom once given,
If we accept, love and honor Him here,
We shall dwell with Him in Heaven.

CHORUS—

SEEK JESUS.

MUSIC BY REV. ROBERT LOWRY.

" Those that seek Me early shall find Me."

SEEK Jesus, seek Jesus,
In childhood and youth,
For they that seek early shall find.
His word hath declared it,
How precious the truth,
The promise how loving and kind.

CHORUS.

Seek Jesus, seek Jesus,
For they that seek early, shall find Him,
He is the true way,
O! do not delay,
Seek Jesus, O! seek Him to-day.

Seek Jesus, seek Jesus,
Ere evil days come,
When thou canst no pleasure obtain,

Lest weary, and fainting,
And longing for home,
Ye wander, and seek Him in vain.

CHORUS—

Seek Jesus, seek Jesus,
While yet He is near,
And He, thy Good Shepherd will be;
His arms shall enfold thee,
From danger and fear,
His life He hath given for thee.

CHORUS—

Seek Jesus, seek Jesus,
While He may be found,
His love, and compassion are free,
And He will receive thee,
Where true joys abound,
For Jesus is seeking for thee.

CHORUS.

Seek Jesus, seek Jesus,
For they that seek early shall find Him,
He is the true way,
O! do not delay,
Seek Jesus, O! seek Him to-day.

POEMS OF TEMPERANCE.

A FOE IN THE LAND.

MUSIC BY PROF. J. W. BISCHOFF.

THERE'S an enemy at hand,
　Shall we forward march, or stand,
While there is within our land a deadly foe?
Foe that charges on the soul,
Lurking in the sparkling bowl,
Luring on to folly, ruin, crime and woe.

CHORUS.

On, on, on, the foe is marching,
　Bearing to death a mighty throng;
Let us rally at the call,
Rally bravely, one and all,
　God is leading in the battle
　'Gainst the wrong.

'Tis a foe with smiling face,
Who with winsome, charming grace,
Binds his victim first with frailest silken band;
But his power will increase,
He will banish joy and peace,
As he holds with fatal grasp, and iron hand.
CHORUS—

Rally for that noble son,
Rally for the precious one,
Upon whom the light and joy of life depend;
Are thy treasures all secure?
Hast thou nothing to endure?
Rally then with tender heart for neighbor—friend.

CHORUS—

Rally with the voice of love,
Bear the emblem of the dove,
Seeking safety from the deluge of despair;
Rally, with your banners high
Waving in the azure sky,
And the eagle's dauntless pinion graven there.

CHORUS—

Forward march, without delay,
Or the foe may win the day,
He is raising new recruits on every hand;
Forward! with the battle-cry,
Those we love may surely die,
If we do not rout the foe within the land.

CHORUS—

"*LOOK NOT UPON THE WINE.*"

"Look not thou upon the wine when it is red. * * * At the last, it biteth like a serpent, and stingeth like an adder."

LOOK not on the wine,
   Though it sparkles so brightly,
And proffers its victims
   Elysian bliss;
For couldst thou but read,
   What it promises, rightly,
The note of its warning,
   Would surely be this:

"Oh! pray that the tempter,
   Forever forsake thee,
Trust not the allurements
   Of brandy or wine,
Lest fearful destruction,
   Shall quickly o'ertake thee,
And death shall enroll thee,
   A victim of mine."

The angel of Pity,
   With sadness, is viewing,
Thy tottering steps,
   Near that fearful abyss,
Where thousands are wild
   Fiery phantoms pursuing,

Where serpents are gliding,
　　Where scorpions hiss.

How fearful the vision!
　　How fatal the real!
Then pause, ere the death-giving
　　Beverage thou sup,
Or thou too, shalt learn
　　That it is not ideal,
To talk of the demons
　　That lurk in the cup.

*TWO TABLES AT THE BANQUET.**

OR, PLEA OF A POLITIC LAWYER.

TWO tables were spread for the banquet,
　　Prepared with fastidious care,
Snowy and spotless the linen,
　　And faultless the elegant ware;
The viands were rich and abundant,
　　Substantial, and fancy, and fine,
Displaying the rarest attractions,
　　Which ladies know how to combine.
There were signs of a conflict with turkey;
　　There were hints of a triumph o'er tongue,—

* Banquet given at the tenth anniversary of law partnership firm.

A conquest so needful for lawyers,
　Retained for the right or the wrong.
In fact all the elegant dainties,
　A generous purse could supply,
Were furnished in lavish profusion,
　To please both the taste, and the eye.
The service of glass, and of silver,
　To all gave a glittering sheen,
Entrancing the eye of beholder,
　A charming and fairy-like scene.
And beautiful flowers were added,—
　The Eden-like touch that is given,
To carry us back to the garden,
　And beckon us onward to Heaven.

All this was in commemoration,
　In modernized tin-wedding plan,
Of man, who in business relation,
　Had ten years, been wedded to man.
Success in the legal profession,
　Had earned them a recognized name,
The firm had abundantly prospered,
　Won fortune, and favor, and fame.
At last, when all things were made ready,
　And the guests, who from far, and from near,
Had come to partake of the bounty,
　And join in the festival cheer,
Were bidden around the two tables,
　So sumptuous, tempting and fine,—
Lo! one was adorned with red ribbon,
　The other was sparkling with wine.

Said the host to the parties assembled,—
(Or thus I'll suppose that he said;
For acts speak a very plain language,
And the wine, and the ribbon are read:)

THE PLEA.

" A Word to explain the adornments,
Which, gentlemen, here you perceive;
We've had a ' Red Ribbon' revival,
A Temperance move, I believe,—
In fact it is really surprising,
The furor this ribbon has made;
It is worn by all classes of people,
Of every profession and trade.
Judge Blank has put on the red ribbon,
For *him*, 'twas a very good plan;
We know that the Judge, for these ten years,
Has been but the wreck of a man;
And yet, he has very fine talents!
When he was admitted, they say,
The judges and bar all predicted,
He'd make a great leader, some day;
I hope he will hold to his purpose,
He's rowing against a high tide,—
I fear he will find in the trial,
He's retained on a very hard side.

" Young Thorp, who last year was admitted,
He could not let liquor alone;
We thought he had gone to the—Dickens,
But he has the red ribbon on;

We thought he disgraced our profession,
　Looked on him with pity and shame;
He's showing he has the true metal,
　And yet may win honor and fame.

" There's Smith, whom we sent up to prison,
　' Best place for the rogue,' people said,
If he had but worn the red ribbon,　　　.
　It might have done wonders for Fred.
At heart he was not a bad fellow,
　But drinking led on to his crime;
I hope he will learn to keep sober, —
　Twelve years will give plenty of time.
And Ryan, and Flynn, and the other,
　All three went for whiskey, you know;
If they all had worn the red ribbon,
　That surely need not have been so.

" And Tyler, the fellow who madly
　The bullet applied to his brain, —
'Tis fearful to think of his conflict,
　With wretchedness, guilt, and the pain,
That led him to welcome the horrors
　Of death, and the gloom of the grave,
To flee from himself, and temptation,
　From whom none were able to save.
'Twas said he was vile, no doubt truly,
　And yet such a death, on the whole,
Proclaims, by a fearful self-loathing,
　There was a fair side to his soul.

For his mother, he left a sad letter, ·
  Said his life had been wicked and wild,
And asked that he might be remembered,
  As he was, when an innocent child;
And added, ' Tell all to take warning,
  If they from the curse would be free,
To *shun the first glass*, for 'twas drinking,
  That brought all this ruin to me;
Forgive all my madness and folly,
  To mend it is useless to try,—
To save further anguish and trouble,
  It is only left me—to die.'

'' Poor fellow! his life was a failure,
  And it is surprising of late,
How often, in very high circles,
  We read of a similar fate.

'' The saddest of all was the woman,
  The suicide, heiress, and bride,
Who left the fair home of her childhood,
  Of luxury, culture and pride;
Who gave all the wealth of affection,
  That lady to lover could give,—
And pictured the future an Eden,
  Where she and her hero would live.
Alas for the fatal delusion!
  Ere the honey-moon passed in its flight,
Her idol lay cruelly shattered,
  And there was revealed to her sight,

A form, so debased and repellant,
    That she, who was gentle and pure,
Sought death, to be free from the presence,
    Which she could no longer endure.
How fresh were the vows at the altar,
    Transforming the maiden to wife,—
The vows, to love, honor and cherish,
    As long as God granted her life.
What pencil can picture the anguish,
    That led to her bitter despair,
When nothing was left her to honor,
    And Love, broken-hearted, was there?
Oh pitiful, pitiful, picture!
    The suicide, heiress and bride,
How worse than alone was her dying,
    Who died by a drunken man's side?
'Tis well for these Temperance People
    To rally, and do what they can,
Against such a terrible evil,
    To woman as well as to man.

'' Now many, for whom it seemed useless
    To labor, or even to pray,
Are taking a turn for the better,
    And wear the ' Red Ribbon' to-day.
' Old Sharp' has put on the regalia,—
    The hardest old toper in town;
Last night he was one of the speakers,—
    They say he just brought the house down;
His wife was the belle of her season,
    And he, the ' best catch,' I am told;

One hardly could think, or believe it,
 To see them, so shabby and old.
The friends of his youth have disowned him;
 She's clung to him all of these years,
And a sad sorry life he has led her,
 In poverty, shame, and in tears.
But now she looks cheerful and happy,
 And truly seems proud of ' Old Ben,'
And says, 'If he only keeps sober,
 He's one of the noblest of men.'

" This will be a good thing for our city,
 We needed a check upon rum,
'Twill do away largely with evil,
 And brighten up many a home;
'Twill lighten the tax on the people,
 For poverty, madness, and crimes,
It will strengthen the hands of true labor,
 And help us to banish hard times.
Still, there are two sides to the question,
 And judges, and lawyers all know,
That to side with a temperance movement,
 For legal men, never would do.
A few of our colleagues have tried it,
 But they will all find, in the end,
That they have lost caste in the market
 Where patronage is the best friend.
One must live by his trade, or profession,
 And liquor men always are free;
The profits so easily gathered,
 They do not begrudge in a fee,—

The State is a splendid paymaster,
　　And she pays the bills for the crime,
That gives us so much occupation,
　　And pays us so well for our time.
Then there are the upright, and sober,
　　Their patronage we must secure,
For such men, for all litigation,
　　Make payment, substantial, and sure.
But here is a fact to make note of,
　　As the current is shown by a straw,
These temperate, good sort of people,
　　Very rarely resort to the law.

"Yes! there are two sides to the question,
　　To please all that we may be able,
We have at the banquet before you,
　　A 'Wine,' and 'Red Ribbon' table:
Remember, this is a free country,—
　　Each man is a king, in his own,
And welcome to do as he pleases,
　　To drink, or to let it alone."

MEMORIAL TREE.*

STAND firmly thou memorial tree
　　Beneath this favored sky;
The memories planted here with thee,
　　Shall never, never, die.

Where winds shall sigh, and birds shall sing,
　　Around our honored dead;
Where sun and stars, their radiance fling
　　Upon their earthly bed;

Thy leaves shall wave, and gently fall
　　Upon the treasure　sod,
Which holds their dust;—but that is all,
　　Their spirits rest with God.

---

* Planted by a delegation from the National W. C. T. U. near the Tomb of George and Martha Washington.

HOME GUARD MEMBER.

I HAVE been to the " Temperance Meeting "
   Of the W. C. T. U.
I went, for a neighbor asked me,
   To see what I could do.
The hardest part was starting,
   For my only way to go,
Was to keep Grace home with the children—
   Nelly, and Fred, and Joe.

As they told what women were doing,
   I thought of the kitchen fire,—
And wondered if Grace would remember
   The bread, and the damper wire.
And when I tried to listen,
   And hear them pray and sing,
I thought of the children and Gracie,
   And if the bell should ring

And a tramp should stand before them,
   Would they be scared alone?—
I tried to think of the meeting,
   But thought much more of home.
I heard one talk of prisons,
   And the Gospel's mighty power,—
I thought of my little prison
   I had left for just one hour.

I listened, and I pondered,
  Till I heard a kind voice say,
" There are many who join our army
  Who must stand home guard all day."
Home guard!   Did I hear rightly?
  That surely must mean me;—
Then she told of the UNION SIGNAL,
  And about the yearly fee.

Another told of THE TEMPLE
  Which to all the world shall say;
" We are working to-day and building
  For a cause that is here to stay."
Another, about the women
  Who have gone across the sea,
Wearing the pure white ribbon,—
  Badge of home-loyalty.

Again I was disheartened,
  I could not join the band—
I had not held in three months
  A dollar in either hand.
And so I left the meeting,
  And thoughtfully went home,
The children had been crying,
  But they laughed to see me come.

I tied up Nelly's fingers,
  That were burned while I was gone;
I got my thread and needle,
  And sewed Fred's buttons on;

I washed the baby's dimples
    And tied his little shoe,
But the tears would fall for thinking
    How little I could do.

When we sat down to supper
    John saw that my eyes were red;
And he said, "Mary you're troubled
    Again with that aching head."
I said, "No, John, but I'm sorry
    There's so little that I can do,—
I would like to join the army
    Of the W. C. T. U."

Then I told about the paper
    And about the yearly fee,
And I said, "John, I've been thinking
    That we might give up our tea."
His voice was very tender,
    As he said, "That will not do,
But you shall join the army,—
    And tobacco I'll—es-chew.

"We will read about the battle,
    As we guard our little band;
But I want you to belong, wife,
    To this army in our land.
So just send in this money
    And put on the little bow,—
You shall be our HOME GUARD member
    Of the W. C. T. U."

THE CRUSADE.

ANSWER TO QUERY: "WHAT HAS THE CRUSADE
DONE FOR YOU?"

WHAT has THE CRUSADE done for me?
  Shown doors of opportunity;
From quiet home of restful ease,
Where friends and self I wrought to please,—
Led out to battle-field sublime;
Displayed new charts for life and time.

As now I glance adown the years,
Recall the songs, the prayers, the tears,
In church, in prison and saloon,
What wonder, there has come so soon
To be one mighty praying band
Whose faith and works circle the land.

As I have read the annals through,—
Recalled the old, received the new
Which span the wonderful decade,
The *then* and *now*, of our crusade;
The record glows with this one thought—
Behold! the wonders He hath wrought.

We're coming at this later hour,
To plead our cause in halls of power;

And while we come with voice of love
Bearing the emblem of the Dove,
We also rear on banners high,—
Our matchless Eagle of the sky.

Shall the proud pinions trail in dust
That hover o'er each sacred trust?
Remember, mightier than the sword,
Is declaration of our Lord,—
The nation which forsaketh Me,
That nation shall forsaken be.

MISCELLANEOUS POEMS.

SIMILES:

LIKE pearls of dew in the bells of flowers,
Like songs of birds in the leafy bowers,
Like the gentle patter of welcome rain,
Falls a soothing word on a burdened brain.

As peace which follows the battle's strife,
Which soothes, yet quickens the pulse of life;
So Charity's voice on an erring heart,
May love for a holier life impart.

Like the first-born blossoms of early spring,
Which smile in the joy and gladness they bring,—
Thus a cheering word may new life bestow,
To a heart frost-bound by Adversity's snow.

As fresh as dew on the thirsty corn,
As fair as the roseate hues of morn,
As bright as stars in heaven's azure blue,
Are the words and deeds, of a friend proved true.

SING. ROBIN, SING.

SING, robin, sing!
Sing at the earliest dawn,
When the shadows of night,
Have taken their flight,
And the beautiful day is born.

Sing, robin, sing!
Sing when the soft perfume,
Is borne on the air,
Freely everywhere,
From the earliest flowers that bloom.

Sing, robin, sing!
Sing when the bountiful rain
Has scattered its pearls
In eddies and whirls,
Sing us thy sweetest refrain.

Sing, robin, sing!
Sing when the waning light
Is bidding thee creep
To thy wing-curtained sleep,
Sing us a gentle "Good Night."

GREEN LAKE.*

BEAUTIFUL waters of Emerald green,
With surface that sparkles in Fairy-like sheen,
With waters that myriads of treasures reveal,
Whose depths keep secure, what they cannot conceal;
How charming thy scenery, so wild and so free,—
GREEN LAKE was a name fitly chosen for thee.

Now glimmering in ripples, at Zephyr's light breath,
Now placid in semblance of Nature's calm death,
Reflecting the splendors of Sol, in his pride,
Inverting the forests that border thy side,
Returning the smiles, of the clouds as they pass,
Transferring their beauty, in Emerald glass.

Of ocean and commerce, thou never hast dreamed,
In thy quiet retreat where kind Nature hath seemed
To place thee to cool heated pulses of Life;
To quell the low fevers, of turmoil and strife,
For those who from business, and care turn aside,
To sport on thy waters, or lave in thy tide.

Since Alchemy failed youth's elixir to find,
The ages succeeding have ever combined,
Endeavors as useless, Life's charms to withhold,
By decking her pathway, with jewels and gold;

* Dartford, Wisconsin; Home of my Father, July, 1872.

Forgetting that lilies, in lovely array,
Outvied a great Monarch in royal display.

Lured on by ambition, men gather their gain,
Oft burdened of heart, and 'neath pressure of brain,
Which turns all the glitter of gold into rust,
Makes coveted diamonds seem worthless as dust,
Until they have learned, what they gathered in haste
For apples of beauty, are ashes to taste.

For such there is rest, on thy banks of repose,
Rare jewels for them, will thy waters disclose,
From the pebbles that lie in their beauty at rest,
To the gold in the lilies that float on thy breast,
While on thy calm surface, from center to shore,
New life may be found in the plying of oar.

Pure blood will flow freely at heart's faithful beat,
A conscience unburdened give sleep that is sweet,
And these shall sustain, amid trial and care,
Through changes that come, in this life, everywhere;
Thus they, greatest treasure, in life shall obtain,
Who keep true heart-vigor whatever their gain.

Adieu lovely waters, so placid and free,
GREEN LAKE was a name fitly chosen for thee;
For green are thy waters, and green is thy shore,
And green shall thy memory remain evermore.

BROKEN CLOUDS.

WHEN do the skies seem brighter
    Than when clouds have broken away?
Or when does the light seem lighter
    Than at early dawn of day?
Or when are the flowers sweeter
    Than they are at early Spring,
When hath passed the dreary Winter,
    And the birds sweet music bring?

And when beats the heart more lightly
    Than when sorrow has fled away,
And the future glistens brightly
    From hope's reviving ray?
What though there are moments of sadness?
    'Tis a beautiful world of ours,
Where we're cheered by hope and gladness,
    Greeted with songs and flowers.

As we sail adown Life's river,
    If the heart be kept aright,
With hope as an anchor ever,
    And love as a beacon light;
Then life may be bright and joyous,
    Though the billows 'neath us roll,
For the Father who reigneth o'er us,
    Will speak peace to the troubled soul.

STORY OF THE LETTER CARRIER'S
OLD SATCHEL.

I HAVE come to report you my labors,
All rusty, and weary, and worn,
My shabbiness speaks of the service,
Which I have so faithfully borne.

Through sunshine, in fair or foul weather,
The patrons we serve have all found,
That Master, and I, have together,
Most faithfully plodded our round.

He bears me strapped over his shoulder,
And yet, I must claim, it is true,
That mine has been half of the service,
In bringing your letters to you.

I often have brought you glad tidings,
Dispelling forebodings and fears;
Again, it has been my sad duty,
To bring you deep sorrows and tears.

But I might not fashion the message,
Which oft I have brought to your door,
I gave what to me was entrusted,
And no one could ask me for more.

My honesty none have disputed,
    For, had I been given to pelf,
The *greenbacks and bonds* I have carried,
    A fortune would make for myself.

Thus, while I retire from the service,
    Much worse for the wear, as you see,
My pockets are empty, and honor
    Untarnished, and conscience quite free.

And my letters! and missives! If only
    Their contents I once should unfold!—
But no, for my service was sacred,—
    Your secrets I never have told.

Perhaps I may venture to tell you,
    How once in my freshness and youth,
I carried such tender love letters,
    Boasting constancy, ardor and truth.

'T was, "Mary, my love, and my darling,
    My own precious sweet, and my dear,
My life would be midnight without you,
    But with you all sunlight and cheer.

"When once we are wedded, my darling,
    Farewell to all trouble and care,
My home can be only an Eden,
    When my beautiful Mary is there.

"How rich I shall be with my jewel,
    Such a pearl to my keeping to give!

We will prove to the world that true lovers,
  Love on, just as long as they live."

That was some years ago, you remember,
  And John and his Mary were wed;
Having told the sweet part of the story,
  Perhaps now, the least—the best said.

Well, John went away on some business,
  And therefore a letter should come
Once more to his sweet darling Mary,
  The pride of his Eden-like home.

I brought it,—her step was less sprightly
  Than when she had met me of yore,
And I thought I saw traces of sadness,
  Where all had been brightness before.

'T was, "Moll, you will look for a letter,
  To tell you when I shall be home;
Can't tell just, but it will be safest
  To look for me—when I may come

"My business is pretty much over,
  But a man must have pleasure you know,
And I, on the whole, have concluded,
  This is just the season to go—

"On a trip to the Falls, and the Mountains,
  With some friends who are going that way;
We look for a jolly good season,
  Can't tell just how long I shall stay.

" Am sorry *you* could not go, Mollie,
   As we used to talk of, you know,
But then,—when a woman has children,
   She could not expect much to go.

" But I had forgotten to tell you,
   That Frank is along with his bride;
He's in luck, and has won a rare jewel,
   In whom he must ever take pride.

" Now Moll, can't you brush up a little,
   Before I shall come back again?
I fear you have grown rather careless,
   A little too homespun and plain.

" Take good care of Ned, and the baby,
   Attend them whatever may come;
Their whooping-cough soon will be over,
   At least by the time I get home.

" I hope you don't need any money,
   But will send you a dollar or so;
This trip will take all my spare greenbacks,
   They're not very plenty you know.

" And, Moll, you will look to the garden,
   Don't let anything go to waste;
Good-bye, I am off to the steamer.
   Your husband, with love and in haste."

*   *   *   *   *   *

This is but a slight intimation
  Of some things in life I have learned,
And leads me to wonder if Mary's
  Love-letters have ever been burned.

Now, after a view so dissolving,
  I think I must tell you of Joe,
Who wrote tender letters to Sally,—
  I carried the first, long ago.

The writing looked shaky, and awkward;
  The name he had written askew;
But his purpose was straight as an arrow,—
  I think I must tell it to you.

"Dear Sally, I'm no letter writer,
  But I have been wanting to tell
A secret, my heart has been hiding,—
  I've loved you long, truly, and well.

"I've no earthly fortune to offer,
  But I have a heart warm and true,
And an arm that is willing to labor,—
  These only, I offer to you.

"If God grants me health, I can furnish
  The needs of a plain humble life,
And I know I should try to make happy,
  One whom I could choose for a wife."

You need not expect I shall tell you,
   The message I carried to Joe;
It made the poor fellow look happy,
   And so you can guess it, I know.

Well,—often I've passed by the dwelling,
   Where Joe made his Sally a home,
And caught the light laughter of children,—
   E'en birds seemed delighted to come,

And add their sweet song to the music,
   That rang on the joy-laden air.
Ah! surely this home was an Eden,
   For "Love in a cottage" was there.

Once Joe was empaneled as juror,
   Which took him a fortnight away,
He wrote such plump letters to Sally,—
   I carried her one every day.

How cheerily came she to gèt them,—
   Their contents you never shall know,
The light in her eye would convince you,
   That these were ', Love-letters"—from Joe.

So Ladies, guard well your heart treasures,
   For I, who was young, and am old,
Have learned that the love the most boastful
   Is surest to wane and grow cold.

FALLING LEAVES.

THE first fading leaves of September,
    Are fluttering downward to earth,
As if they would bid us remember,
    That death follows quickly on birth.

So recently waving in beauty,
    Responding to each summer breath,—
Now falling, in humble leaf duty,
    To teach us the lessons of death.

They whisper and sigh as they tremble,
    As if to their comrades to say,
" ' Tis useless for us to dissemble,
    You shortly must follow this way.

" The bright days of summer are over,
    And we, who hung high in our prime,
Have been but the first to discover,
    That leaves must all wither in time.

" You may cling till the frost gives you warning,
    By chilling your veins with the cold,
Your green tints of summer all turning
    To crimson, and purple, and gold.

"In those brilliant hues, though you glory,
    Your fate is the lot of us all,
Repeating the often told story,
    That leaves in their season must fall."

THE DYING YEAR.

'TIS the last lone hour, of the dying year,
    And the winds are sighing, low and drear,
As they toss the sleet, half snow, half rain,
In a farewell dirge, 'gainst the window-pane,
As I listen to hear the gladsome shout,
"The New Year in, and the Old Year out."

No one grieves for the Old Year's death,
As they wait for his latest, failing breath;
For now, that his glory and prime are o'er,
He may go, as the years have gone before,
Where the bells of Time are joyfully rung,
O'er the birth of the New Year, fresh and young.

Yet gladly we hail thee! bright New Year,
With words of welcome, and songs of cheer;
When spring-time, summer, and autumn are past,
Old winter shall grizzle thy beard at last,—
And thou, when thy glory and prime are o'er,
Shalt go, as the years have gone before.

The years they come, and the years they go,
While Time, with a tide of ceaseless flow,
Is bearing us over life's changing hours,
Now under the shadows, now 'mid the flowers,
But ever anon, toward Eternity's shore,
Where Time, with his changes, shall come no more.

OLD BACHELOR AND POLLY.

(*IN DIALOGUE.*)

"HERE I come back to my dismal old room,
No one to pleasantly welcome me home,
No one to say, 'I am glad you have come,'
    No one to greet me, but Polly."

POLL PARROT—
    "*How-dy-do?   How-dy-do?*"

"'Pretty well, darling,' is what I should say,
If,—well, no matter, 'tis many a day
Since I have thought of things just in that way;—
    'Pretty well, thank you, old Polly.'"

POLL—
    "*What's the news?   What's the news?*"

"Nell, whom I flirted with,—long ago wed;
Clara I promised,—poor girl, she is dead;

Widow Bland jilted me, and, it is said,
 Married a worse fellow, Polly."

POLL—
 "*Pretty Poll! Pretty Poll!*"

" ' Pretty ? ' Ah no! you're *not* pretty, but—well—oh!
There should be *some one* to speak to a fellow;
Though you are stupid, and greenish, and yellow,
 Still you can speak to me, Polly."

POLL—
 "*Polly's sweet? Polly's sweet?*"

" ' *Polly's sweet!* ' No! that you certainly are not;
And it is evident too, that you care not
Whether I come or go, only you fare not
 Well in my absence, old Polly."

POLL—
 "*Polly want a cracker,—Polly want a cracker.*"

" ' Polly wants' something, you always are saying;
Keeps me quite busy, your bills to be paying;
But no fine dress I must buy, for displaying;
 That is quite good of you, Polly."

POLL—
 "*Poor Polly! Poor Polly!*"

" ' Poor Polly;' now you talk just like a woman;
Surely, old Polly, this is a bad omen;

Fretting and whining gives comfort to no man;
   This is all foolishness, Polly."

POLL—
      " *Polly's sick—Polly's sick.*"

" 'Polly's sick!' now you say that to get petting,
Just like a woman, made sick by your fretting;
Will you have blisters, bleeding, or sweating?
   What shall I do for you, Polly?"

POLL—
      " *Call Missus—Call Missus.*"

" 'Call Missus!'   Poll, *I have called her*, for years,
Called her with coaxing, and pleading, and tears,
Faithfully called, yet no Missus appears;
   Can you ask more of me, Polly?"

POLL—
      " *Kiss Polly—Kiss Polly.*"

" 'KISS POLLY!'   Now you just try to be witty;
There's not a soul, but you, in the whole city,
To take a kiss from me—more is the pity,—
   But here's a kiss for you, Polly."

POLL—
      " *Polly'll tell—Polly'll tell.*"

"*Hush*, you old bird! this is no time for joking,
Give me no more of your tiresome croaking,

Now hush your racket, while I go to smoking,
You are a nuisance, old Polly.''

POLL—
    "Boo-hoo-hoo! Boo-hoo-hoo!"

'' There now! you're acting, again, like a woman,—
Strange that a *bird* should be so nearly human,—
Here is some candy, Poll, from your old Tru-man,
    Now wipe your tears away, Polly.''

POLL—
    '' Polly's sweet ? Polly's sweet ?''

'' ' *Polly's sweet ?* ' Yes, Deary, sweeter than honey;
Couldn't be bought—*or sold*, for any money,—
Again like a woman! now isn't that funny ?
    Now go to sleep, pretty Polly.''

POLL—
    '' Ha-ha-ha, Ha-ha-ha.''

SOLILOQUY.

'' Isn't it strange there's so much in a word,
Whether to cat or dog, pony or bird ?
So 'tis with WOMAN,—at least I have heard;
    I can judge only by POLLY.''

BUMBLE BEE AND CLOVER.

M R. Buzzing Bumble Bee
Said to Blushing Clover,
"You're as sweet as sweet can be,
May I be your lover?"

Said Miss nodding little Clover,
Unto Bumble Bee,
"You're a handsome, honest lover,
Just the one for me.

This was in the morning sunny;
Ere the day was over,
He had stolen all her honey
And forsaken Clover.

DAWN.

IN amber slippers, the princess Dawn
  Trips out on the eastern sky.
Queen Night with her sable trail sweeps on
  As the king of Day draws nigh.

Thus on, and on, 'neath changing skies
  Their ceaseless march they keep;
The king with his stern command to rise,
  The queen with her wand of sleep.

The charming grace of her star-lit face
  The king can never have seen,
Though he follow on at a kingly pace,
  Fair Dawn comes ever between.

SUNNY HOURS.

"I MARK ONLY THE SUNNY HOURS."

(Inscription on an ancient sun-dial.)

A S the sunlight gleams and glimmers
        Through the shadows of the trees;
As some melodies are wafted,
    By the storm and on the breeze;
As some blossoms smile in beauty
    By each rough and rugged way,—
Thus the joys of life are given
    With each earth-revolving day.

Seldom are the weeds so tangled
    But some flowers meet the view;
Seldom is the sky so darkened
    But some light is gleaming through;
Seldom is the heart so burdened
    That it has no ray of bliss,—
Let us cull the best and brightest,
    In a life as brief as this.

Let us learn of the sun-dial
    But to mark the sunny hours;
Pass with care the thorns and briars,
    Seeking for the humblest flowers;
And when shadows gather round us,
    Drape our joys as with a shroud,
May we trust the sacred promise,
    "There is light beyond the cloud."

"JACK LIGHTFOOT." *

"The war horse."—Job xxxix, 19th and 25th verses, inclusive.

HOW many a heart would be gladdened,
   If all the true things which are said,
Might fall on the ear of the living,
   Which never can waken the dead.

Not so with this VETERAN CHARGER,
   For all one might write or might say,
Would give the old hero less pleasure,
   Than a ration of oats or of hay.

And yet, for a service so faithful,
   So valiant, untiring and long;
It is meet that we offer a tribute
   In true "In memoriam" song.

Right proudly he bore his commander,
   Where'er he was bidden to go;
He never retreated from danger,
   And never turned back from the foe.

---

* "There was a notable funeral at Des Moines, Iowa, the other day. Old Jack, the last of the war horses of the rebellion, was buried with military honors, and about fifty veterans followed him to the grave and left upon the mound of earth floral tributes to his memory. He carried Colonel, afterwards General Geddes, through nearly fifty battles, and was always eager, intelligent and fearless. Jack never learned to retreat. To the day of his death the sound of martial music thrilled him, and he was ready to respond to the bugle-call."—*Chicago Mail.* March, 1890.

Delighted at sound of the cannon;
The battle he smelled from afar,—
Whenever he heard martial music
Jack Lightfoot was ready for war.

He never applied for a pension,—
To grumble he never was known,
Yet Jack received loyal attention
In a "Soldier's Home" * all of his own.

Brave Lightfoot has won his last battle,
And to music of drum and of fife,
Been laid to rest under the daisies,
Discharged from the warfare of life.

We talk, write and sing of our heroes,
But how much the nation may owe
To Jack, for his speed, nerve and daring,
The nation saved,—never may know.

---

*Jack was left to the care of Captain James Miller, of Des Moines. For twenty-two years the horse marched in every Memorial Day and Fourth of July procession in Des Moines. He was petted and admired, and treated to the best that Captain Miller could afford.

OUR FATHER'S CARE.

WE praise our Father's loving care
    And magnify our graces,
Whene'er our skies are bright and fair,—
    Our paths in pleasant places;
Yet oft upon life's changing sea
    When heavy waves are rolling,
We tremble and forget that He
    Is at the helm controlling,

Who holds the lightning in His hand,
    Who gives the voice to thunder;
Who rears the mountains high and grand,
    And spreads the valleys under;
And yet, who heeds the sparrow's fall,
    And ceaselessly is keeping
A tender watch-care over all,
    In waking or in sleeping.

When dark storms gather o'er the way
    We wisely may remember,
While each year has its blooming May,
    Each has its drear December.
Yet frost and snow shall not abide,
    For ceaseless change discloses,
The coming of the fair Springtide
    With all her wealth of roses.

TRAILING ARBUTUS.*

M Y heart is strangely moved to-night
By this love-bearing token;
As if a ray of golden light
In ecstacy had broken,
Through clouded sky to simply tell
The sun beyond was shining,
Proclaiming truth we love so well,
That clouds have silver lining.

When trials fill the passing day,
Kind acts seem the completer;
When thorns are springing in the way,
Bright blossoms seem the sweeter.
And thus this fragrant little gift
Comes with a double duty,
A curtain from my sky to lift,
And to reveal its beauty.

Perchance I ne'er in life may meet
The friend who sent the token;
The missive brought a message sweet,
Although no word was spoken.
And thus I wing these lines to say,
If e'er they find the giver,—
May flowers brighten all thy way
And LOVE ABIDE FOREVER.

* Received anonymously by mail.

THE OLDEN TIME.

IN olden times, ere daughters went
From the parental home,
To kindle fires upon the hearths,
Which each might call her own,
The neighbors used to gather in
And needles deftly ply,
In quilting diamonds, hearts and stars,
To please the tasteful eye;

Indulging oft in quiet jest,
About the coming wedding,
While blushes singled from the rest,
The maiden at whose bidding
The merry quilting bee was made,
And neighbors all about,
Joined in so cheerfully to give
The lass her "setting out."

In those days mothers didn't buy
Rare velvets, silks and laces,
But always gave a good supply
Of sheets and pillow cases.
For portiere or lambrequin,
For them 'twas very certain,
That pretty chintz was good enough
To make a stylish curtain.

The chandelier with radiant gleam,—
  They did not know about it;
But tallow dip with milder beam,
  Did just as well without it.
With snuffers bright to trim the light,
  Brave lovers did not falter,
Nor maidens shrink their troth to plight,
  Upon Love's changeless altar.

By dancing flames of open fires,
  Where bright andirons glisten,
The fancied pictures love inspires,
  An artist might not fasten;
They had no gems by Raphael,—
  That mattered not at all,
Where "sweet home" pictures were within,
  Not hung upon the wall.

Thus, for our worthy ancestors,
  John, and his charming Mary;
Rare bric-a-brac and statuette,
  Were quite unnecessary;
Unused to fuss and feathers
  It was their opinion that
Pretty birds were made for singing—
  Not to wear upon the hat.

Of diamonds, Mary only knew
  The diamond which expresses,
The love of warm hearts quilted in
  To scraps of pretty dresses.

This gave a value all untold
  Unto the patchwork olden,
When pewter served as silverware,
  And brass was good as golden.

They made no wedding-gift display,
  Which often means to borrow
What one can not afford to-day
  To bè returned to-morrow.
But churn and reel, and spinning-wheel
  Would quietly be carried,
With kindred treasures to their home
  Soon as the twain were married.

Then, winsome Mary did not need
  A courtly "maid of honor,"
To train her trail, undo her veil,
  In state, to wait upon her.
They just walked simply side by side
  And pledged at Hymen's altar,
Where lover won a helpful bride,
  The lass——not a defaulter.

MORNING IN THE COUNTRY.

THE fields are all over,
    White dotted with clover,
So recently darkened and still;
    Where bees are now coming,
    With musical humming,
Their honey cups eager to fill.

    Each brown little fellow,
    Tinged lightly with yellow,
In diligent search may be seen;
    His errand so sunny,
    To find bread and honey,
And carry it home to his queen.

    The sun is distilling
    Dew diamonds, and filling
The air with a fragrance most sweet;
    Bright jewels adorning
    The paths of the morning
Where Rest and Activity meet.

    The gay Morning Glories
    Are whispering stories
To butterflies burnished in gold.
    " Pink, purple, or pearly,
    We wake bright and early,
Our fairy-like tents to unfold."

With russet breast swelling,
Cock Robin is telling
His mate it is time to arise;
  The lark was before him,
  Is now soaring o'er him
And flinging his song to the skies.

The swallows are flitting
And darting, or sitting
To chatter fresh news to their wives;
  The ducks have awakened,
  Their morning bath taken,
The greatest delight of their lives.

The cattle are lowing,
And leisurely going
To pastures inviting and green,
  While singing, and turning
  From milking to churning,
Fair Molly, the milkmaid, is seen;

While Robert, her lover,
Goes on through the clover,
To harvest field, gleaming like gold,
  And as she is singing
  Love's echoes are bringing
His whistled "sweet story of old."

Oh! roseate dawning
Of life's early morning!
Go sing with the lark, while ye may;

Soon thou wilt be nearing
The twilight, and hearing
The nightingale's soberer lay.

JEALOUSY.

(*DIALOGUE SONG.*)

ARABELLA—

"NAY! do not speak!—'tis all in vain!
I've learned you love another;
I saw you meet her at the train
    While waiting for my brother.
I saw the quickly stolen kiss,—
    Hands clasped with eager pressing,
A glance which could mean only this,
    A heart throb of caressing.

"A tender vine is confidence,—
    When tendrils once are broken,
No act can e'er make recompense,
    No word that can be spoken,
Will make them twine so lovingly
    As though they ne'er were severed;
This charmèd tie for you and me
    Is broken now forever.

"I thought your heart was all my own,
    When first our troth was plighted;

'Tis well its faithlessness was known
　Before we were united.
For when I pledge in Hymen's bans,
　In life ne'er to be parted,
It must be with a noble man,—
　A lover single hearted.

"And now, farewell! This foolish tear
　Will wash away my sorrow,
And I shall rally,—never fear!
　And wear a smile to-morrow.
I'll pray for blessings from above
　On one so fondly cherished;
But good-bye, to the former love
　From this hour it has perished."

REGINALD—
　"Aha! my love! my sweet! my own!
　　And have you thus been grieving,
　Because I loved another one,
　　As you were fain believing?
　I met her at the train 'tis true,
　　And also true,—I kissed her;
　Would you forgive me if you knew
　　The darling was—my sister?

　"And dearest, my poor aching heart
　　Has been itself deceiving,
　I saw that handsome man depart,
　　Just as the train was leaving.

You passed me by and took his arm,
    I thought you loved another,
And now I find my wild alarm
    Was all about—your brother.''

ARABELLA—

    '' Forgive.''

REGINALD—

                '' Forget.''

ARABELLA—

                    '' 'Tis very plain
        That we have been mistaken.''

REGINALD—

    '' And shall we e'er conclude again
        That each has been forsaken?''

ARABELLA—

    '' At least, my love, I promise this
        When you and I shall marry,
    That you your sister Belle *may* kiss,''

REGINALD—

    '' And you—your brother Harry.''

READING.

THERE are some debts which gold can pay,—
Others, that one must owe, alway;
Of these, for value that has been
Dropped from the point of priceless pen.

The graceful form of poesy
Hath ever a sweet charm for me;
Some buds and blossoms I entwine
In simple wreaths,—and call them mine.

I may not cross the ocean's main,
Or scale the Alps, or roam the plain,—
May ne'er behold Rome's sculptured halls,
Or gaze on ancient ruined walls.

And yet in my secluded home,
The varied lands of earth I roam;
So quickly roam, and back again;—
My faithful guide, the trusty pen.

Earth's gilded ways I may not know,
Her jewels come, and flash, and go;
For this abiding joy I plead,
Give me mind, heart, and time to read.

THOUGHT PICTURES.

I CLOSE my eyes, and yet I see
    Scenes beautiful and bright;
The fairest visions come to me
    In darkest hours of night.

And do you ask what magic wand
    Such imagery hath wrought?
I answer, that the master hand
    That paints for me, is Thought.

He bears me o'er the boundless main,
    Without fear of disaster;
And past the fleetest lightning train
    He flashes even faster.

Then borne in magic diving-bells,
    I plunge beneath the sea;
Where amber, pearls and rarest shells
    He quickly paints for me.

I scale with him the mountain high,
    Without a fear of falling,
Then bound to burning crater nigh
    To view its depths appalling.

Borne on the wings of passing cloud,
   I sail through azure skies,
And shower pearls to thirsty worlds
   Where fairest verdure lies.

On phantom wings far, far away,
   To lands I ne'er may see,
Thought bears me, and in grand array
   Spreads out their scenes for me.

I cross with him the mystic tide
   Which hath an unknown shore;
Soon anchor on the golden side
   And roam its city o'er.

The pearly gates are open wide,
   And, rapture! there I see
My loved and lost ones glorified,
   Waiting to welcome me.

In all the vast redeemed throng
   Within that city fair,
Not one is idle, yet not one
   Is burdened with a care.

In mansions fine, through charming bowers,
   Or by life's sparkling tide
We wander 'midst the fairest flowers,
   And I am satisfied.

I hear the songs that angels sing
   Around the Father's throne,

Then back to earth rare pictures bring
  Of Heaven, all my own.

Aided by all I've read or known,
  With wondrous fancy wrought;
I thus hold pictures, all my own,
  Transcribed, impressed by thought.

A DREAM.

OR, WHO STOLE CLARA?

STRANGER, have you seen our Clara?
  She was here but yesterday;
Laughing, prattling in her cradle,
  While I watched the dimples play;
With a mother's fondest fancy
  I interpreted her song,
And she made our home a castle
  Where the bars of love were strong;
But some one has stolen Clara,
  Have you seen her in the throng?

*   *   *   *   *   *

Now I mind me! She was larger,
  And went merrily to school;
Carried flowers to her teacher,
  With her basket, slate and rule.
But I have not seen her coming
  From the school in many a day,

And my eyes are dim with watching,
  And the evening sky is gray.
Some one must have stolen Clara!
  Have you met her on the way?
*   *   *   *   *   *
I mistake,—she was a maiden,—
  (It is strange I should forget!)
And she filled our home with music
  Where I seem to see her yet;
Tall and graceful, fair and gentle,
  Sunny as a cloudless day,
Sweetest girl in all the country,
  I am sure sir, you would say;
But some one has stolen Clara,
  And has carried her away.

"Why," you ask me, "do I think so?"
  Why! I've hunted here and there,
In the nursery,—chamber,—garden—
  And can't find her anywhere.
And my sun will soon be setting,
  For my hair is turning gray,
And I want to find my darling—
  What is that, sir, that you say?
"Father Time, and a young lover
  Must have stolen her away?"

What sir! you! *you* were the robber?
  And the lady by your side
Is my daughter?—It *is* Clara,
  And you stole her for your bride.

"Sweetest girl in all the country,"
Thus "*you* thought as well as I,"
Can I "blame you that you stole her
When *that* was the reason why?"
Truly sir,—you quite confuse me,
For how can I make reply?

* * * * * *

"Wake up! Ganma; oo's been deamin',
And been talkin' in 'oor seep,"
And I woke, to find my darlings,—
Clara's babies, at my feet.

A SONG OF SEVENS.

TO JOHN G. WHITTIER ON HIS SEVENTY-SEVENTH BIRTHDAY.

OF the rarest and fairest of rhythmical gems,
  Which the author has lavishly given;
'Mid the brightest to shine in her diadem,
  Is Jean Ingelow's "Song of the Seven."

How faithfully painted, her pictures of life,
  From its dawn, until shadowy even,
Child, maiden, bride, mother, and widowed wife,
  All shown in her seven times seven.

But thine is a truer, more beautiful song,
  Unto whom hath been graciously given,

The power, life's melody still to prolong
Even on to thy SEVENTY-SEVEN.

Its chords shall reëcho again and again,
Though thy harp be laid silently down,
For children unborn, shall take up the refrain
Of the songs that have won thee renown.

MAUD MULLER will rake in the meadow the hay,
Dream of joys that may never be given;
The Judge will sigh on, in the "might have been" way,
Long after thy seventy-seven.

DAME FRIETCHIE will wave her loved banner on
high,
With a courage born only of Heaven,—
Unnumbered with heroes; yet ready to die,
Ere our flag to its foes should be given.

With the sword of the pen thou hast valiantly fought,
Fearless words for the right ever spoken;
A nation has followed thy beckoning thought,
And the fetters of slaves have been broken.

May thy days still remaining be restful and long;
May thy sky glow the brightest at even,—
When sunset is past, thou shalt waken to song,
In the beautiful mansions in Heaven.

NEIGHBOR AND I.

MY neighbor's charming home I see,
   With stately tower above it;
And then the hardest law for me,
   Is this, "Thou shalt not covet."

My cottage is so plain and bare;
   His palace walls are shining;
My days are pressed with toil and care;
   In ease he is reclining.

My eyes are dim, I cannot see
   Why constant wearing labor,
Should press so heavily on me—
   So lightly on my neighbor.

*   *   *   *   *   *

Such was my plaint, one year ago;
   My neighbor was concealing
The dark, consuming, fearful woe
   His life is now revealing.

Thus, while I saw his shining gains,
   I did not know his losses;
I could not feel his secret pains,
   Or bear his hidden crosses.

My sleep was sweet, though I was borne
    Daily upon care's billow;
I did not know about the thorn
    Within my neighbor's pillow.

Beside the crosses that we bear,
    If we could measure other's,
We should unneeded pity spare,
    From lighter burdened brothers.

While often those who seem to be
    Earth's choicest blessings sharing,
Would claim our tender sympathy,
    For sorrows they are bearing.

We see some shining ship afar,
    With sails and banners flying,
But may not know what burdens are
    Down in the deep hold lying.

I would not dare exchange my own,
    My hopes, my joys, my labor,
For jeweled crown and gilded throne
    And, sorrows of my neighbor.

EASTER LILIES.*

YE beautiful Lilies of Easter!
   Your mission is two-fold to-day:
To gladden the hearts of the many,
   Who gather to worship and pray;—
Proclaiming a risen Redeemer,
   Who burst through the mould and the gloom,
And rose in a beauty resplendent,
   Light-crowned, from the depths of the tomb.

Again, on a mission most tender,
   Borne away from the gaze of the throng,
To a chamber of languishing trial
   Ye come, like the breath of a song;
Proclaiming a risen Redeemer,
   By beauty and fragrance most rare,
Who had borne for us, sorrow and anguish,
   A heavenly home to prepare.

Ah! beautiful Lilies of Easter!
   Inspiring to anthems of praise!
Ah! beautiful Lilies of Easter!
   The languishing spirit to raise
Through faith, to the risen Redeemer,
   O, teach us a lesson of trust,
To look to our glorified Master,
   Away from the tomb and the dust.

PORT JERVIS, April 6, 1890.

* Brought from the sanctuary to the sick room.

THE EAGLE'S NEST.

"As the eagle stirreth up her nest."—Deut. xxxii, 11.

THE eagle stirreth up her nest,
 Compelling use of pinions
Destined to bear a dauntless crest,
 Over earth's broad dominions.
For real,—but not seeming good,
 The mother bird is bringing
To brink of crag her timid brood
 Despite their helpless clinging.

In all this seeming cruelty,
 She tenderly is caring,—
Urging her eaglets first to fly,
 Then swooping down and bearing
A frightened fledgeling on her wings,
 Above the depths appalling,
Then safely back to eyrie brings
 Her charge, from fear of falling.

And thus again, and yet again
 She presses to endeavor;
Stirs up the nest, that lulls to rest,
 Yet aids and watches ever
Until she sees each peerless bird,
 So famed in ancient story,
Soar from the nest her love had stirred,
 An eagle in its glory.

COMPENSATIONS.

THOUGH my dwelling were a palace,
    And my fortune wealth untold,
And my couch were draped in damask
    Curtained round with lace of gold;
These could not assure the comfort,
    While the stars their vigils keep,
Which is granted to the cotter
    With his toil-rewarding sleep.

(Eccles. v, 12.)

Though my board were spread with viands
    Costliest that wealth could buy,
And my service were the rarest
    Art and nature could supply;
These could not command the relish
    Which attends the humble spread,
Where tense nerve and sweating forehead
    Win and sweeten daily bread.

(Ps. cxxviii, 2.)

Though my coach were richly cushioned
    And my "Coat of Arms" should be
Recognized throughout a kingdom,
    And declare high pedigree—
These could not impart the vigor
    Which the sturdy toilers know,

As they follow in the furrow,
Gleaming plowshare, to and fro.

(Eccles. v, 18.)

They who soar to high achievement
In the charming realm of song,
Mount not there by idly dreaming,
But, toil wearily and long.
Myriad notes must die in silence
Ere the world is thrilled with joy,
And the struggling toiling singer,
May the heaven-born gift employ.

They who carve the noblest statues,
Must the hardest rock conform
To the soul's unseen ideal,
Eloquent in grace of form;
When at last, the work completed
May the world's applause command,
God hath furnished skill and marble,—
Man, the chisel-wielding hand.

Ere the "masterpiece" in beauty,
On the canvas may unfold,
It must fall from brush immortal
On the canvas of the soul.
And whate'er the picture painted,—
Simplest flower, or mountain high,
Every tint, or light or shadow,
Must be gathered from the sky.

Thus hath toil her compensations,
  And the talents that are given
Double only by their using—
  Gain on earth, to gift from Heaven.
Wealth, to bless must yoke with labor,
  Toil, to bless must win reward,
And the master and the servant,
  Both find pattern in our Lord.

ANTE AND POST MORTEM.

L ET us serve the living present,
      Which will quickly pass away,
Waiting not for grand to-morrow,
  Serve in trifles of to-day.
Often has the pulse been quickened,
  And life's failing fountain stirred,
By a gentle act of kindness,
  Or a single loving word.

If we turn unto the poets,
  Of great Homer it was said:
"Him who begged his bread when living,
  Seven cities claimed when dead;"
And that by his tragic dying
  Only, were due laurels won
For the rare undying genius
  Of the poet, Chatterton.

Better far to cheer the living
    Than to praise or mourn the dead;
More to life than shaft of marble,
    Is the pillow for the head.
More to heart Love's faithful token,
    Making all its joy complete,
Than a costly mausoleum,
    When its pulse has ceased to beat.

Have we loving words to offer?
    Let them carry solace now;
Have we fragrant flowers to gather?
    Let them grace the living brow.
We shall serve our loved ones better,
    If we do not blindly save
Treasure stolen from life's pathway,
    To be strown upon the grave.

"Dust to dust." It is but "ashes,"
    And whate'er one's living powers,
Dust shall yet through Nature's courses,
    Nourish rootlets for earth's flowers.
Let us brighten all life's journey,
    Heaven hath robes and mansions fair,
Let us fill the earth with music,
    Angel choirs are singing there.

Let us carve upon the marble
    Of the monument of Time,
Pictures fair of Love's devotion;
    Records of a life sublime.

When this fleeting life is ended,
    And we reach those mansions fair,
Just and true will be the record,
    Angels have engraven there.

THE COURT OF THE MUSES.

A COLLOQUY,

PREPARED FOR YOUNG LADIES' ENTERTAINMENT.

CHARACTERS.

Nine Muses.

1 Calliope.	4 Euterpe.	7 Urania.
2 Clio.	5 Erato.	8 Thalia.
3 Melpomene.	6 Terpsichore.	9 Polymnia.

Two or More Attendant Fairies.

GUESTS.

Spring.	Morning.
Summer.	Naiad.
Autumn.	Fashion.
Winter.	Dissipation.
Fame.	Temperance.
Night.	Liberty.

DRESS.

Muses—Simply attired in white. Broad sashes, with name of each Muse in gilt letters, gives a pretty effect.

Fairies—Young misses in white or very light pink. May be arrayed according to fancy. May have miniature wings.

GUESTS.

SPRING—With ornaments and gifts of flowers.

SUMMER—Flowers, and grain.

AUTUMN—Autumn leaves, and gifts of fruit.

WINTER—Mantled in white, with frosted hair.

FAME—Richly dressed, but plain.

NIGHT—A brunette, with flowing hair, robed in black,
    ornamented with stars.

MORNING—A blonde, robed in light pink, with imitation
    dew-drops.

NAIAD—In simplest robe of green, bearing pearls, shells,
    and water-lilies.

FASHION—Gaudily attired, with grotesque fashions of the
    past made prominent.

DISSIPATION—Dressed in garnet.

TEMPERANCE—In white, or pale blue.

LIBERTY—Large fine figure, with plain rich dress.   Must
    be draped in, or bear the American flag.

MUSIC.

Music may be either vocal, or instrumental, by the
Muses, or others summoned to their aid.

The dress of characters, the music, and the effect of
the Colloquy, must depend largely upon the taste of those
having it in charge.

MUSES ASSEMBLED IN COURT.

ENTER FAIRY.

FAIRY—Gracious Muses, there are guests in the
outer chamber, awaiting admission into thy Celestial
Court.

MUSES—IN CONCERT—

Welcome to the Muses' home,
Any who may hither come,
Bearing tokens of their worth,
To the children of the Earth.

FAIRY—Spring cometh, asking audience of the
Muses.

MUSES—ALL—

We will welcome gentle Spring,
If some token she will bring,
Which shall prove her real worth,
To the children of the Earth.

ENTER SPRING—

Fairest of flowers I bring to thee,
Weave now I pray thee, a rhyme for me.

MUSE 1ST—

Bright and beautiful form of Spring,
Gladly we greet thee again;
Fresh and fair are the flowers ye bring,
Decking each hill and plain.

MUSE 3D—

Gems of beauty are everywhere seen,
Scattered from thy rich urn;
The fields thou art robing in mantles of green,
In token of thy return.

MUSE 6TH—

Gladly we list to the songs of birds,
   Which ever rejoice in thee;
Their blithesome notes of welcome are heard,
   In every bower and tree.

MUSES—ALL—

Then gladly we all, at this joyous time,
   Will welcome thee, beautiful Spring;
And gaily we'll weave thee a garland, in rhyme,
   In return for the flowers ye bring.
Rest awhile with our joyous throng,
And list to the notes of a Fairy song.

*Attendant Fairy takes the gift and places it upon
a receptacle for gifts.*

MUSIC.

ENTER FAIRY—Summer cometh also, and crav-
eth admittance.

MUSES—ALL—

Summer cometh after Spring,
Some fair token she must bring,
Which shall also prove her worth
To the children of the Earth.

ENTER SUMMER—

The golden grain I ripen for thee;
Both fruit, and blossom, accept from me.

MUSE 5TH—

Summer, brightest of the seasons,
  Welcome 'midst our joyous train;
We accept thy worthy off'ring,
  Crown, entwined with golden grain.

MUSE 4TH—

Spring has brought us fairer blossoms
  Than we find within thy bowers;
Yet we know that Summer's brightness,
  Can alone mature the flowers.

MUSE 8TH—

May Earth's children all remember,
  When the golden sheaves they bind,
That the harvest fast is passing,
  And the Summer soon will end.

MUSES—ALL—

Glad we greet thee, radiant Summer,
  Tarry now amidst our throng;
And in token of thy coming,
  We will give a greeting song.

Attendant Fairy takes the gift.

MUSIC.

ENTER FAIRY—Hither cometh Autumn, who also desireth admittance.

MUSES—ALL—

Thou may'st also usher Autumn,
    If some token, rich in worth,
She shall bring, which shall proclaim her
    Welcome messenger to Earth.

ENTER AUTUMN—

Richest of fruits I bring to thee,
Hast thou a cluster of rhymes for me?

MUSE 8TH—

Welcome, richly laden Autumn;
    Tempting token thou dost bring,
Which must win thee ready welcome
    From a peasant, or a king.

MUSE 4TH—

Thou hast painted a fanciful garment
    For every bower and tree;
In return for thy diligent labor,
    We will weave a bright Poem for thee.

MUSES—ALL—

Glad we greet thee, glorious Autumn;
    Richest praise to thee belongs,
Linger yet within our palace,
    While we honor thee with songs.

Attendant Fairy takes the gift.

MUSIC.

ENTER FAIRY—Winter cometh, seeking favor
of the Muses.

MUSES—ALL—

> We will freely welcome Winter,
>> If some gift she bring to prove
> That she, like her sister Seasons,
>> Comes in mercy, and in love.

ENTER WINTER—

> A garment of purity bring I to thee,
> Sing now I pray thee, a song for me.

MUSE 3D—

> Thou art called *relentless* Winter;
>> We have heard of thee of old,
> And they say thy breath is chilling,
>> And thy heart is dead, and cold.

MUSE 9TH—

> But the story I believe not,—
> Forms so beautiful deceive not;
>> I will give thee all thy due;
> I admire thy sparkling brightness,
> And thine ample robe of whiteness,
>> Sure must warm, and nourish too.

MUSE 1ST—

> Still, thou teachest all a lesson,
>> Which shall prove thy real worth,

Brighter than the flowers of spring-time,
Richer than the fruits of Earth.

MUSE 7TH—

Would the child of Earth remember,
The Great Giver but for thee?
Would he learn to prize the blessings,
Which are lavished, full and free?

MUSES—ALL—

Glad we greet thee, faithful Winter,
Muses e'er will truthful be,—
List to tones of richest music,
Which we give to honor thee.

MUSIC.

ENTER FAIRY—Fame awaiteth admittance.

MUSES—ALL—

Bid her enter, if she bear
Worthy token, rich and rare.

ENTER FAME—

I bear the names of the children of Earth,
Who have reached a pinnacle grand;
Not mines of gold, nor royal birth
Admit to my wonderful land;
Though his course be brief, yet he liveth in rhyme,
Who beareth my magical name;
He never dies on the shores of Time,
Whose name is enrolled by Fame.

MUSE 7TH—

Thy land is indeed a wonderful land,
Yet alas! for the child of Earth,
Who toils to reach thy pinnacle grand,
If he has not personal worth.

MUSE 2D—

From the peasant in his cottage,
To the king upon his throne,—
His life's in vain who toils for Fame,
And seeks her praise alone.

Third Muse takes the scroll from Fame and reads.

SCROLL OF FAME.

Strange names are written on thy scroll,
    Here is one famed for song,
And that is well, but here is one
    Famous for crime, and wrong.
One is made famous by his wit,—
    Another for his learning,
Just by a critic, famous for
    His wonderful discerning.
Here is a famous traveler,
    A hero of renown;
And here a famous fiddler
    Just by a famous clown.
And here are famous poets, some
    Who died from maddening wine;
Favored by Muses, yet they served
    As slaves at Bacchus' shrine.

And here are famous statesmen,
  Who framed *infamous* laws;
And also famous orators,
  Who wakened loud applause.
And here are famous clergymen,
  Honored for noble lives;
And here a bishop, famous for—
  A score or more of wives.

MUSES—ALL—

Enough! enough! the scroll of Fame
  The Muses must disown,
Until thou bearest us the name
  Of the good and great, alone.
                              [EXIT FAME.]

ENTER FAIRY—Night cometh, and would see
the Celestial Muses.

MUSES—ALL—

Welcome to our spacious hall,
Night, enrobed in darkest pall.

ENTER NIGHT—

Stars and rest I bring to thee;
Hast thou a soothing rhyme for me?

MUSE 2D—

Rest thou bringest for the careworn,
  Dearer gift than all beside;
Quiet to the weary spirit,
  With the hours of eventide.

MUSE 7TH—

> Starry gems are brightly shining
>> On the sable brow of Night,—
> Dearer to a band of Muses,
>> Than a gorgeous crown of light.

ENTER FAIRY—Morning cometh also desiring a token from the Muses.

MUSES—ALL—

> Bid her welcome to our palace,
> Muses love to greet the Morning.

ENTER MORNING—

> I have fled away from the bowers of Night,
> To bathe my form in dewy light;
> Health and vigor I bring to thee,
> Hast thou a wakening rhyme for me?

MUSE 8TH—

> Fair, angelic form of Morning,
>> Oft we've met thee on thy way,
> Rosy light thy brow adorning,
>> Herald of a brighter day.

MUSE 4TH—

> Sparkling dew-drops deck thy mantle,
>> Flowers yield thee sweet perfume,
> Birds pour forth their sweetest anthems,
>> When thy rays their bowers illume.

MUSIC.

ENTER FAIRY—Naiad cometh, desiring admittance into thy gracious courts.

MUSES—ALL—

>   Bid her enter, if she bringeth
>   Treasure from the sparkling tide.

ENTER NAIAD—

>   From the mountain brook, where the lilies grow,
>   I have gathered pebbles bright;
>   Then borne along by her ceaseless flow,
>   Through the summer lands of light,
>   I have added fairest shells and pearls,
>   Till I reached the boundless sea,
>   And there I have gathered countless gems,
>   And bring them all to thee.

MUSE 1ST—

>   Thou hast brought us rare and precious gems,
>   · From the rivulet, brook and sea;
>   On the shore of the Muses' Fairy-land,
>   We will gather pearls for thee.

MUSE 5TH—

>   These pearls we will weave with fancies bright,
>   In the graceful form of rhyme;
>   Which shall float on the rolling sea of thought,
>   To the shores of every clime.

MUSE 9TH—

>   We will tell of the rubies and shells, that deck
>   Thy palace, beneath the blue sea;

We will tell of the beautiful Nymphs who weave
  Bright emerald robes for thee.

Attendant Fairy receives the gift.

ENTER FAIRY—Fashion waiteth.

MUSES—ALL—

  Fashion! Fashion! who is she?
  Bid her enter, we will see.

FASHION ENTERS.

MUSE 2D—

  Is that mortal? is it human?
  Surely it can not be woman?

MUSE 5TH—

  Fashion, we are told thy name is;
  Prithee, tell us what thy claim is?

MUSE 3D—

  What is thy pretended worth,
  To the children of the Earth?

FASHION—

    I am ever coming
      With something new,
    Giving the ladies
      Something to do;
    Now painting their faces,
      With tints so rare,

Thus making the plain
  And sallow, fair.
I bleach their hair
  To make it white;
Or dye it black
  As the wing of Night;—
If they are bald
  I soon procure,
And crown their need
  With a fine coiffure.

What good do I do?
  Why, I venture to say,
The belles of the land,
  If they had their own way,
Would grieve less at heart,
  Should they happen to fail
In the style of their beaux,
  Than the cut of their trail;
The beaux may carouse,
  Drink, gamble and swear,
They will overlook trifles,
  But show greatest care
In the swing of the trail,
  Or the frizz of their hair.
The gents all admire me,
  And that, I suppose,
Is the reason the ladies
  So dote on my clothes.
The gents will laugh,
  And the charge deny;

Yet one can see,
  With but half an eye,
In the fit of the boot,
  In the shape of the hat,
In the cut of the coat,
  In the tie of cravat,
They're very careful,
  All the while,
To follow Fashion,
  And keep in style.
Of a stylish wife,
  Each man is vain,
But thinks his neighbor's
  Should be more plain.

What good do I do?
  Why the thought is absurd,
For you, gracious Muses,
  Must surely have heard,
That we might as well,
  Without trail, frill, and sash on,
Be out of the world,
  As out of Fashion.

MUSE 1ST—

        Distorted in figure.

MUSE 4TH—

        Bepowdered in face.

MUSE 3D—

        Bereft of all beauty.

MUSE 5TH—

        Devoid of all grace.

MUSE 7TH—

> If all thy followers
>   Make such a show,
> Then out of the world,
>   They might as well go.

MUSES—ALL—

> The Muses deny
>   Thy arrogant claim,
> Let "Fashion and Folly"
>   Henceforth be thy name.

ENTER FAIRY—Dissipation waiteth admittance.

MUSES—ALL—

> Bid her enter, we shall see
> What *her* proffered gift will be.

DISSIPATION—

> I come, I come, with the sparkling wine,
> From the purple fruit of the cheering vine;
> Come drink of the nectar, I bring to thee,
> Thou surely wilt love it, and welcome me.

MUSE 1ST—

"Look not thou upon the wine when it is red;
* * * At the last it biteth like a serpent, and
stingeth like an adder."

DISSIPATION—

> Oh! I have a retinue long and grand,
> Which I lead to a beautiful, charming land.

They care but little, and seldom look
In the musty pages of that old Book;
Then drink and be merry, drink and be gay,
Drink, and drive dull care away.

MUSE 3D—

"Woe unto him that giveth his neighbor drink."

MUSE 7TH—

Thou leadest, at first, through a charming land,
   Yet danger, though hidden, is there,
For the brink of ruin lies just beyond,
   And the valley of dark despair.

MUSE 4TH—

"Wine is a mocker; * * * Whosoever is deceived thereby is not wise."

DISSIPATION—

      In Halls of splendor,
        I walk with pride,
      With wealth, and beauty,
        On either side.
      In Courts of grandeur
        They welcome me,
      And praise the gift,
        That is spurned by thee.

MUSES—ALL—

Man may praise thee, if he chooses,
But thou canst not bribe the Muses.
        [EXIT DISSIPATION, HAUGHTILY.]

ENTER FAIRY—Temperance cometh also.

MUSE 1ST—

>   Will she bring us gift to spurn?

MUSES—ALL—

>   Bid her enter, we will learn.

TEMPERANCE—

>   This Crystal draught from the wayside spring,
>   O Muses, is all the gift I bring;
>   Pure as the sunlight, free as the air,
>   I bear it with gladness, everywhere.

•   MUSES—ALL—

>   Welcome, welcome, doubly welcome,
>   With thy gift, so pure and free;
>   Thine indeed a blessed mission,
>   And we gladly honor thee.

MUSE 6TH—

>   Sparkling in the mountain brooklet,
>   Gurgling in the lowly glen,
>   Dancing, glancing, everywhere,
>   Dearer than Earth's jewels are,—
>   Nature's crowning diadem,—
>   That is what you bear.

MUSE 4TH—

>   Leaping in the fountain,
>   Glist'ning in the dew,

Falling in the raindrops,
Ever fresh and new;
Bounding in the waterfall,
Rolling in the river,
Telling ever of the love
Of a Gracious Giver.

MUSE 9TH—

It quelleth fever, it quencheth thirst,
It makes the bud and the blossom burst,
It nurses the rootlets underground,
Wherever a living plant is found;
It falls from the heavens, in bountiful shower,
It flows from deep caverns, with ceaseless power,
It spreadeth the seas, and the ocean grand,
Which bear Earth's children to every land.

MUSES—ALL—

We'll echo thy praises, again and again,
Thou bountiful gift to the sons of men.

MUSIC.

Temperance song, in praise of water.

ENTER FAIRY—Liberty asketh admission to thy
Celestial Court.

MUSES—ALL—

Bid her enter if she brings,
Gift as bright as crown of kings.

ENTER LIBERTY—

I come! I come! with a broken chain,
Emblem of torture, and fear, and pain.
Wherever I go, oppressers flee,
Their shackles are all unclasped by me.
Hither and thither I haste to save
The fettered king, or the abject slave.
No crown I bear, with jewels rare,
But manhood I save from the spoiler's snare.
With heart unfettered I come to thee,
Hast thou a song for the brave and free?

MUSES—ALL—

Aye! our choicest, sweetest rhythms,
We will gladly give to thee;
We admire thy noble bearing,
And we love the brave and free.

MUSE 9TH—

Haste, on Eagle's pinions soaring,
Unto those who, aid imploring,
    Long for thee in every land;
In thy mission bright and glorious,
Mayest thou ever be victorious,
    Breaking every tyrant's band.

MUSE 7TH—

Glad the morning sun shall meet thee,
And the stars of Night shall greet thee,
    With their cheering silver rays;

Thy loved name shall live in story,
Twined with brightest wreaths of glory,
Gemmed with richest gifts of praise.

MUSES—ALL—

Let Temperance, and Liberty,
Now rally, hand in hand,
United should their mission be,
To every fettered land.

Temperance and Liberty clasp hands, and are crowned by the Muses.

MUSE 1ST—

The bright flowers of Spring-time
Shall circle thy brow.

Liberty kneels, or bows, to accept the wreath.

MUSE 8TH—

The harvest of Summer,
I give unto thee.

Temperance receives the wreath of grain, and flowers.

MUSE 5TH—

The rich fruits of Autumn,
Accept from me now.

Liberty receives the basket of fruits.

MUSE 3D—

> While I will bestow
> The rich gems of the sea.

*Bestowing necklace of pearls, corals, or shells,
upon both Liberty and Temperance.*

*Salutation of the Muses, to which each Guest in
turn bows graciously in response.*

MUSES—ALL—

> Hail to the Seasons!
> And Morning!—and Night!
> Graces we give unto thee.
> Hail! to thee, Naiad,—
> And Temperance bright,
> And Liberty, noble and free.

*The Guests move as if to retire from the Court,
but are detained.*

MUSES—ALL—

> Linger yet; this happy throng,
>   Let no thought of parting sever;
> Till we give a cheering song,
>   Wishing Joy and Peace forever.

MUSIC.

*" Star Spangled Banner," or a song of general
joyfulness.*

With closing line Curtain falls.